PSYCHIC SOCIALITE STORIES BY JANE SEVIER

Fortune's Fool
A Billy Sunday Kind of Love

A BILLY SUNDAY
KIND OF LOVE

A PSYCHIC SOCIALITE STORY

JANE SEVIER

ISBN-13: 978-0615704975

ISBN-10: 0615704972

http://www.janesevier.com/

Cover art and book design by April Martinez

DEDICATION

In memory of John Houseman, who was one of my heroes.

ACKNOWLEDGMENTS

I am grateful to Lisa and Howard Patterson, whose friendship and encouragement keep me going when I'm not sure I can. Stalwarts Rae Ann Parker, Rosalind Paul, and Rochelle Staab read this book as a manuscript, and their insights were invaluable. April Martinez designs the most beautiful book covers in the world. Thank you all.

CHAPTER 1

Memphis, 1933

When Calpurnia Waters volunteered to let the Amazing Waldo make her disappear, she never dreamed it would be for good.

Master conjurer and disciple of the mysteries of the most ancient of sorcery and magic, the illusionist came to the Bluff City "Direct from the grand stage of the Hippodrome in New York!," as his posters proclaimed. In these hard times, dozens of Memphis men thanked him for the three days of work it had taken to raise his vast tent on the fairgrounds, spread cubic yards of fresh sawdust under it, stock it with hundreds of wooden folding chairs, and suspend the multitude of twinkling lights under which the magician now performed.

Suave in tuxedo and white tie, his Douglas Fairbanks mustache neat and his inky hair slicked back smooth against his skull, the Amazing Waldo held his audience spellbound. He had already transformed a rabbit into a dove and transported his leggy assistant Matilda to the very back of the audience from a box on the stage that he had stuck swords clean through, changing the color of her spangled outfit from crimson to gilt for good measure. On this September Saturday afternoon, every one of those folding chairs was filled, and every man, woman, and child in them strained forward to see what miraculous illusion or legerdemain would come next.

"Now, good people of Memphis assembled here, are any of you so daring as to risk being transmuted into energy, transferred to another dimension, and then restored to the fellowship of your rejoicing family?" Waldo said from the front of the stage.

He motioned to Matilda, who with the help of two burly stagehands wheeled an enormous Egyptian mummy case to the center of the stage.

"Who among us here tonight would not embrace immortality?" he said. "From the dawn of time, the promise of eternal life has enraptured mankind. Untold ages ago in the storied valley of the Nile, the ancient Egyptians prepared their dead for the afterlife. To earn a place on the great god Ra's boat for the journey to the land of the Two Fields and that everlasting life, they believed the bodies and organs of the departed must be preserved. They would need them again after their souls traveled safely through the underworld."

Waldo stepped to the case and rested his hand against its side.

"First, the heart of the deceased had to pass scrutiny in the hall of the goddess Ma'at, who placed it on a balance to be weighed against a feather. To board Ra's boat, one's heart had to be light. Only the kind, the gentle, and the upright who spent their lives doing good were light of heart."

He stalked back to the edge of the stage and regarded the now-quiet crowd.

"Those whose hearts could not pass Ma'at's test were denied a place on Ra's boat and vanished from the face of the earth forever." He struck the spot over his heart with his right fist. "Now, I know that there must be many among you who live virtuous lives. This antique case once housed the body of a great pharaoh, a king wise and good who no doubt found his rest in the afterlife." Right palm now open, he gestured toward the case. "Which of you is willing to enter?"

The crowd stirred. This time, fewer hands went up than had appeared when the Amazing Waldo first issued his challenge.

———

CALPURNIA TURNED TO HER FRIEND HATTIE TAYLOR WHERE THEY SAT on the second row of the colored section. "I'm going." Calpurnia waved her hand in the direction of the stage.

"Cal, what on earth makes you think he's going to pick you?" Hattie gave her a you-have-clean-lost-your-mind grin.

"This right here." Calpurnia tapped the brace on her right leg. "You know it's always better if he can get a crippled girl up on the stage. Makes the audience feel sympathy."

Hattie snorted. "Honey, it's been a good while since you were a girl. And how is he supposed to know you're crippled? You know he can't tell that all the way over here. "

Calpurnia elbowed Hattie. "Hush, and help me up. I'm going to step out into the aisle. And anyway, he's a magician, isn't he?"

"All right." Hattie shrugged and handed Cal her two canes just like the ones Mr. Roosevelt used. She braced herself with them, rocked forward onto her feet from her seat at the end of the row, and shuffled sideways until she stood in the middle of the aisle. There, she waited for the conjurer to notice her, the only woman standing in the colored section.

THE AMAZING WALDO GAZED OUT OVER THE AUDIENCE, MANY OF THEM languorously waving paper fans decorated with pictures of Jesus knocking at the sinner's door that Watkins-Fish Funeral Home had handed out at the entrances. Memphis was still warm in September, and with all the humanity crammed in under the tent, it got hot even with the sides opened at intervals to let the air in.

"Are there so few who dare?" he said. He stretched out his hand and swept it to encompass all the audience. "No strong young man eager to prove his valor? Come, there is nothing to fear. I thought the proud people of this city were made of sterner stuff than this. "

Around the audience, a few more timid hands had gone up. At the back, a group of teenage boys stood, jostling each other, whether competing for notice or perhaps doing their best to push their friends forward, he couldn't tell. Waldo locked eyes with a sassy-looking blonde in the middle of the crowd. She smirked at him as though to say, "I know what you're up to." He was tempted to call on her, but the hulk next to her with an arm around her shoulders discouraged him.

Then, he saw her. A frail Negro woman, a cane in each hand, standing erect and quiet to the far right of the stage. She would do, and bringing her up would shame all the country yokels whose girlfriends and wives pushed them toward the stage while they pretended to be too sophisticated to consider such foolishness. Waldo crossed to the stairs, strode down them to the woman's side.

"Think you're up to it?" he asked her in a low voice.

"Yes, sir."

Waldo threw his hands in the air. "At last, our intrepid volunteer. I will escort her to the stage to face the perils of the unknown. Matilda, prepare the chamber."

The magician's assistant pulled open the front of the mummy case, entered, tapped the sides to show they were solid, and walked out again, waiting while Waldo and the volunteer made their way up the steps and across the stage. The woman's gait was deliberate, the tap of her canes on the wood floor marking her progress. The clamor that had greeted her died down so that by the time she reached the case, there was complete silence.

Waldo faced the audience again. Removing the black star-bedecked cloak he had draped over his shoulders, he whirled it over his head and let it fall into a fan shape at his feet. "This mantle once belonged to a master of the occult arts, a mage so powerful that it is said that at his death, not only did his immortal soul cross over but his mortal body did as well, leaving behind only this cloak, a papyrus so ancient that it crumbled at the touch of my hand, and this ring."

Turning the back of his right hand toward the crowd to reveal what appeared to be a gigantic ruby set in an ornate gold-and-enamel band, Waldo stretched his left arm out at a right angle to his side. Gradually, he extended his right arm as well until he seemed about to embrace the crowd. "As the one true heir to that power, the cloak and the ring passed to me. I will call upon their power to make Miss . . . ." He turned to the petite woman waiting by the case.

"Calpurnia Waters."

". . . Miss Calpurnia disappear. Are you ready?"

"Yes, sir."

"Then, let us begin." Waldo reached into the case and rapped with considerable force on the sides, again showing that they were solid. He clapped his hands twice, and Matilda appeared at his side with a mask and strips of cloth. "You afraid?" he whispered to Calpurnia, who shook her head. He winked at her. "I've got you."

"Not only did the faithful of the Egypt of yore believe that one must be light of heart, but they were also convinced that they must preserve the body after death if the departed were to achieve immortality. Thus was born the art of mummification, an art so grisly to our modern ears that I shall refrain from explaining it out of deference to the ladies in the audience and to any gentlemen who may be particularly delicate of constitution."

He held out a hand to Matilda, who placed in it the mask.

"When the body was prepared, it was bandaged in strips of clean linen like those the lovely Matilda now holds aloft in her hands, but we will spare our courageous Miss Calpurnia that ordeal." He lifted the mask toward the crowd. "No doubt you have all heard of the fabulous treasures of King Tut discovered in the legendary Valley of the Kings not so very long ago. As he slept in his royal tomb, Tut wore a golden mask and rested in a case protected by sorcery like the one that awaits Miss Calpurnia here. The mask I hold in my hand is an exact replica of the one that safeguarded Tut through the millennia. I will now place it over her face to ensure that she, like that ancient pharaoh, will be returned to the light of day."

With the mask in place, Waldo picked up his cloak from the floor and draped it over Calpurnia's shoulders. Taking one of her canes, which he passed to his assistant, he grasped her now empty hand and gestured for her to enter. Calpurnia hobbled in, turned to face the crowd, and braced herself against the back. Waldo released her. He and Matilda stepped to either side of the case.

"Matilda!" Waldo said.

His assistant swung the cover of the case closed and latched it. Waldo struck the front with the ring. "Can you hear me, Miss Calpurnia?"

"Yes, sir," came the muffled answer.

"Then I will strike the case three more times before I open it again."

"Yes, sir."

Over his shoulder, the Amazing Waldo gave the audience a long look. It was as quiet as a churchyard under the tent. He raised his right hand over his head and swung it down sharply so that the crack of the ring striking the wood echoed throughout the space. He struck it a second time, and a third. Then he gazed out over the crowd again, arms stretched over his head.

"Are you ready?"

"Yes!" an old man somewhere in the middle yelled out, and everyone laughed.

"Matilda!"

The assistant unlatched the case and swung the lid open again. It was empty, except for the magician's cloak, which lay in a puddle at the bottom. There was a gasp from several quarters. Waldo snatched up the garment to reveal the gold mask, which he held up to show to the audience before he handed it to Matilda. With his mantle draped over his arm, he stepped into and out of the case and walked around it, tapping the sides. He crossed to the front of the stage, swirled the mantle over his head, and let it fall to his shoulders before he bowed deeply.

The crowd erupted into applause.

No one clapped louder than Hattie Taylor.

Standing in the near darkness at the back, medium Joseph Calendar did not applaud.

"And, now," said the Amazing Waldo, "to return Miss Calpurnia to her loved ones."

This time, he closed the lid of the case himself. He rapped it once and opened it.

There was no one inside. He paused ever so briefly before turning a brilliant smile on the house. He closed the case and struck it three times as decisively as he had to make Calpurnia disappear. But when he opened it again, it was still empty. Behind him came murmurs and the sound of people shifting in their seats. He turned to face them.

"There's nothing to worry about, my friends. It seems Miss Calpurnia is reluctant to return from the other realm, so we will wait for her to do so on her own terms." He closed the lid again, exchanged a glance with Matilda, and nodded slightly.

She crossed to a stand at the side of the stage and brought back a long, latched box, which she opened and held out to Waldo. From it, he withdrew two ornate curved swords that glinted under the lights.

"Now," Waldo said, "who will allow me to pass these ancient scimitars through his body? Completely without harm, I assure you."

Chapter 2

As long as the show people would allow her to, Hattie waited for Calpurnia inside the tent. When they came to shoo her away, she marched backstage to ask the Amazing Waldo what had happened to Cal. He was polishing one of the swords from the act while Matilda fed a cage full of white doves.

"She has simply chosen to remain in the other realm," he said, waving a hand to dismiss Hattie and her question.

Hands on her hips, she gave him a look that told him what she thought of that theory. "Don't tell me you don't know where she is."

"I'm sorry. Maybe she walked home."

"Walked home. Now, you know there is no way on earth Calpurnia Waters walked home. You still got one of her sticks right there." Hattie pointed to the cane leaned against a table behind the magician. "Even using both of them, it was hard enough for her just to make it up onto that stage. You need to get up out of that chair and help me find her right this minute."

"Look, maybe she took a cab. It happens sometimes after the illusion. It's pretty dark inside the mummy case, and people decide they're not getting back in. If your friend is the least bit afraid of close spaces, she might have decided to stay backstage. She's probably home waiting for you. Now, I've really got to get ready for tonight's show. I hope you'll come back."

He went back at the sword with his polishing rag.

"She wouldn't leave without letting me know. I am not moving one step from here until she either comes in looking for me or you tell me where she is."

Waldo returned one of the scimitars to its box and fastened the lid. "All right. We'll go over every inch of this stage and tent, but I promise you that your friend is not here."

They walked up and down each row of seats, crawled up under the stage, and walked all the way around the outside of the tent in the fading light, but there was no sign of Calpurnia. Waldo even opened the still-empty mummy case for Hattie again and showed her the trap door the missing woman had been lowered through to the space under the stage.

"Look, I've just showed you how the illusion works, and for all I know, you're going to tell every living soul in Memphis now. Would I have done that if I had any idea where your friend went? She could have slipped past the stagehands without anyone seeing her."

"Wasn't there somebody up under there to push her back up into the case for the rest of the miracle? She couldn't have climbed up in there by herself."

Waldo rubbed the back of his neck. He called the hands out on the stage and quizzed them about Calpurnia. Each denied that it had been his day to work the mummy case.

"So, what you're saying is that nobody was under the stage for the trick?"

Glancing sideways at one another, they all shook their heads.

"I ought to fire every last one of you." Waldo turned to Hattie. "I don't know what to tell you. Either one of these worthless idiots is lying, or your friend managed to get herself out of there somehow."

"I'm sitting right here and waiting for her." Hattie crossed her arms and positioned herself on one of the magician's trunks.

"Suit yourself, but you'll have to clear out once we're ready for the next show."

After Waldo and Matilda finished preparing for the evening performance and went off to find themselves some supper, Hattie waited outside for another hour. From the phone booth in the drugstore on the corner across from the fairgrounds gates, she finally tried calling Cal's house. No answer. On the way home on the trolley, she grew more frantic by the moment over the idea of Calpurnia alone somewhere in the dark.

———

BACK HOME AT THE MARCHAND MANSION, WHERE SHE WORKED AS cook and housekeeper, Hattie sat at the kitchen table with Nell Marchand.

"Something has to have happened to her," Hattie said. "It just isn't like her to leave without telling me she was going home. And nobody is answering the phone at her house. Her mama is deaf as a post, but usually if I let the phone go on ringing long enough, she'll hear it at last and pick up. Course, she can't hear half of what you say when she does, but I can generally holler loud enough for her to understand me."

"I tell you what, Hattie, if you're that worried, why don't we have Jenkins run us over there before supper?" Nell said. She finished icing the cake Hattie had made and licked the caramel off the spatula before she put the utensil in the sink. "I bet you anything it will turn out that Calpurnia is so tired that she did decide to take a cab, and she's asleep and not hearing the phone either. Or maybe she and her mama went out somewhere."

"Huh. Calpurnia Waters doesn't ever spend a dime on anything if she can help it. Every now and then, she will go to the picture show if I promise to buy the pickles or candy. That's how I know for sure Cal didn't take any taxi home. She's too tight with her money."

"All right then, we'll go see about her."

In a neighborhood peopled by domestics who worked in big houses in fancier parts of town and by owners of small businesses around Beale Street, the driver Jenkins pulled the Duesenberg up in front of Calpurnia's house, which was dark and still. Nell made him go up to the front door with them, not because she was afraid but because if they found something awful, she wanted another set of hands to deal with it. The chauffeur knocked so loudly that it stopped just short of rattling the door off its hinges. No one answered.

"Jenkins, go around back, please, and see if there are any lights on. Maybe they're in the kitchen and just can't hear us."

In less than a minute, the driver returned. "No, ma'am, Miss Nell. Doesn't look like anybody's home."

"See?" Hattie said. "I've just got a bad, bad feeling about this. I'm going to step next door. Sometimes, Miss Ruby plays cards over there, and they may know something. You and Mr. Jenkins might scare everybody, so wait here on the porch, please."

Hattie was back in a flash, shaking her head. "They said Miss Ruby went with one of the ladies from our church to sit with a friend at the hospital. They don't know what time she'll be back."

Nell patted the cook's arm. "I bet Calpurnia will be in Sunday school tomorrow, and you can fuss at her then about worrying you."

"What if she's not?"

"If she's not, then we'll see what we need to do about it. Meanwhile, let's go home and have some of that caramel cake that Miss Bess eyed all day. She won't touch a bite until we're there to have it with her."

Nell turned to go, but Hattie remained rooted to the spot, staring at the front door as though willing it to fly open.

"Hattie, we're not doing any good standing out here in the dark. Maybe Cal went to the hospital, too, or is waiting somewhere for her mother to come home. If she isn't at church tomorrow morning, I'll phone Sargent Acker and see what he thinks we ought to do. All right?"

"I just know something bad has happened to her. She's not any bigger than a minute, and it's not like she can defend herself. She always acts like she's got two good legs, just like everybody else, but if somebody were to get after her, she couldn't even . . . ."

"Even run away."

Hattie nodded.

Nell put her arm around the cook's shoulders. "I'll call first thing in the morning if we still haven't heard anything."

———

NELL MARCHAND WAS MORE CONCERNED ABOUT CALPURNIA THAN SHE would admit to Hattie. That the cook herself was worried was enough for Nell. Hattie Taylor never fretted about anything, had never worried to speak of in all the time Nell had known her, which was all her life since she and Hattie had been born on the same day in the same house. Even when Nell's no-count husband Ellis died and she discovered he had left her penniless, Hattie had remained calm and taken charge of the household until Nell hit on fortunetelling as Madame Nelora as a way to make money.

Sociable, practical, dependable Hattie knew half of Memphis. But Calpurnia was special to her, perhaps because she was as self-sufficient as a person as handicapped as she was could be and perhaps because when she did ask for help, it was from Hattie that she asked it. Hattie Taylor liked doing for people.

On Sunday morning, Nell called the Waters house, but there was still no answer. She sent Hattie to Sunday school in the Duesenberg so Jenkins could bring her straight back if there were no sign of Calpurnia. Hattie usually took the trolley, and Jenkins drove Nell and her mother-in-law to church, but if Bess Marchand could forgive her for making them miss their own Sunday school classes this once, surely the good Lord would, too.

Nell heard the car pull in under the porte cochère, and her heart went down to her toes. She hurried to the kitchen door.

Hattie came in wiping her eyes. "Nell, she—"

"I'm picking up the phone right now." Nell raced to the front hall where the telephone lived and asked the operator to connect her with Arnold Acker in Germantown. She was inordinately relieved when he answered on the second ring.

"Sergeant Acker, please forgive me for disturbing you at home and on a Sunday morning, but Hattie is so upset about a friend of hers who seems to have gone missing that I felt it was best to call you right away."

"Miss Nell, I would say it's a pleasure to hear from you, but not with bad news like this. Would you like me to come by your house and talk to Hattie?"

"Would you, please? I hate to make you miss church, but I'm quite concerned myself. Please apologize to your wife for my bothering you at home."

"Marta understands. Well, maybe not understands exactly, but being married to a Memphis police sergeant for 20 years, she at least knows things are bound to happen on the weekends, too. I'll be over there as quick as I can."

CHAPTER 3

Lounging in the parlor of his lavish suite at the Peabody Hotel in downtown Memphis, the Amazing Waldo thought that of all the advantages his success as an illusionist had brought him, he appreciated luxury the most. Born Waldo Peterfreund in Sandusky, Ohio, he might have ended up a railroad engineer like his father and passed his days covered in soot and grit had he not received a magic set on his eighth birthday. Forever more, he would be grateful to the maiden aunt who that day had planted the seeds of this life that fit him so well. There was nothing like savoring a cocktail in his private quarters after a performance to remind him of that.

"I wish you would get rid of that damn cat," Matilda Nowak said to Waldo. "Do you have any idea how hard it is to find hotels that will take cats?"

He stroked the head of a golden-eyed, obsidian-black feline that had leapt up onto the arm of his chair and thrust her sleek head under his hand, demanding attention. "Sekhmet has been with me longer than you have, my dear Matilda, longer than you can imagine. I couldn't begin to fathom going on without her."

"Sometimes I think you'd rather have her in the act than me."

"Sometimes I think I would, too. Sekhmet doesn't complain nearly as much as you do, and I suspect that her pedigree is more distinguished. Now be a good girl, and pour me a couple of fingers of that gin. Tonight's crowd took a lot out of me."

"Yeah, well the cat doesn't have to make all the traveling

14

arrangements, wear those stupid sparkly things on stage in front of a bunch of slobbering yahoos, do two shows every Saturday and Sunday, and act as your bartender every night. If she did, she might complain a little, too."

As though she understood not only that she was the subject of the conversation but what was being said about her, the cat gave an odd, off-key yowl and stalked from the room, head and tail held high.

"Now, you see what you've done, Matilda? You've offended Sekhmet, and she'll probably sulk for days. You know how terribly sensitive she is."

"I'll find her a nice, fat mouse to make up for it." Matilda poured two stiff drinks, dropped three ice cubes in each, and came to sit across from Waldo. "How much longer you plan for us to be on the road? I haven't seen my folks since last spring, and I told Ma I'd be home for Christmas. It's bad enough that I have to miss the World's Fair."

"I'd think you'd welcome the chance to spend the winter here in the lovely warm South rather than in frozen Chicago. I don't think I'll ever get last winter's chill from the wind off the lake out of my bones."

"I like the cold. And I miss Ma's kielbasa and kraut."

"I tell you what. The house is dark tomorrow night. If there's a Polish restaurant anywhere in Memphis, we'll go have kielbasa and kraut."

Although not exactly mollified, Matilda looked slightly less put out. Because petulance seemed to be her native state these days, Waldo had developed the ability to judge it by degrees. For Matilda, tonight's mood might almost pass for contentment. He never should have taken her out of Back of the Yards, should have left her there to marry a fat butcher and raise a houseful of chubby children, but she had been young and star struck and wanted to see the world, so he had given in to the temptation.

Her dark nature aside, she was a good and capable assistant. She was getting a little long in the tooth, though, and before too much time, he'd have to find someone younger and fresher to wear the spangles she claimed to loathe. And then there was the antipathy that she and Sekhmet had felt for each other from the moment they had first clapped eyes on each other. The cat bore it with more dignity than did his aide-de-camp, but Waldo felt her keen displeasure. Perhaps he should permit Sekhmet to choose the next assistant rather than allowing his libido to rule his choice.

"You know, my dear, if you have wearied so of travel, then perchance you should think of going home to your family. You're still young, and if you want children of your own, time is running short for that."

Matilda jumped up, spilling her drink and almost overturning the cocktail table in the bargain. Waldo rescued his gin at the last moment.

"I knew it," she said. "I knew you were getting tired of me. Now you want to throw me away like I was nothing. What happened? See some blonde tootsie in the audience tonight? After everything I've done for you, after I gave you my best years, you're just going to toss me aside." Matilda wailed and ran from the room, slamming the bedroom door behind her.

Waldo could hear her sobs through the door, imagined that half the hotel could hear her. He sighed and took another sip of his drink. Sekhmet emerged from whatever hiding place she had retired to and climbed onto his lap. He scratched her behind the ears, and she purred, a strong, soothing rhythm that drowned out some of the woman's weeping.

"Yes, my treasure," he said to the cat. "I think it is time for Matilda to go back to Chicago. Shall we try it on our own for a while again, hmmm? That might be best, at least until we can find someone suitable."

Sekhmet licked the back of Waldo's hand, settled herself more comfortably, and drifted off to sleep.

THE NEXT MORNING, THE CAT AND THE MAGICIAN BOTH SLUMBERED ON the sofa when Matilda emerged from the bedroom, suitcase in hand,

and flicked the lights on. She shook Waldo by the shoulder until he opened a apathetic eye to look up at her.

"This just isn't working no more, Waldo," she said, slipping into the native patois that he had worked so long and diligently to rid her of. "You're right. I'm goin' home. Pop keeps telling me he's got a place for me in the shop when I'm ready. And who knows? Ma said Andy Kowalski always had yen for me, and now that his mother's dead, he'll be needing a wife to help out."

"Godspeed, then, Matilda," he said, not bothering to get up from the sofa. "Have enough money for your train passage?"

She smiled a bitter smile. The bastard really had no heart. "Yeah. I been saving up, just in case. I should have listened to Pop when he told me you was a rat and not to trust you." She picked up the suitcase and opened the door. "So long." She looked back at Waldo. He had rolled over to face the back of the sofa and seemed to have gone back to sleep. Matilda clicked off the lights and stepped out into the hall, closing the door quietly so as not to disturb the other guests. "Yeah, so long," she said again, this time quietly because there was no one to hear her anyway.

CHAPTER 4

At the next performance, Joseph Calendar was among the audience again when the Amazing Waldo announced that he would extend his Memphis run and move to the Odeon Theatre indefinitely while he interviewed applicants to replace his assistant Matilda, who had been called home to her family unexpectedly just that morning. This announcement displeased Calendar. Displeased him greatly. The less he saw of Waldo, the more he liked it, and as far as he was concerned, the conjurer had already darkened the door of Memphis much too long.

It was not that he feared competition from the Amazing Waldo. For all his flash and flair, the illusionist did not dabble in communications with the spirit world, and Calendar's practice as medium to Memphis society was established and secure. Rather, he felt a different kind of menace from Waldo Peterfreund, an enmity that went back as far in time as did Joseph Calendar's memory.

"Who dares come to the stage to join me and share in the mysterious learning of the ancient East that I have gleaned from mages and sages over a lifetime of study?" the conjurer said. "I can promise you a life of adventure, of travel. You will see the wonders of the world, from the ancient temples of Abu Simbel to the cafes of Paris."

A boy Calendar judged to be about 15 stood and waved his hand. "I'll go, mister."

The boy's father jumped up beside him and shoved him back down into his seat. "No, you ain't," the man said. "You got chores to do."

The audience laughed.

"That's a generous offer, young man," Waldo said, "but I need the feminine energy of a female assistant." One jaunty eyebrow lifted, he paused and smiled out over the crowd, which responded with more chuckles and titters. "Perhaps one day you may elect to study the magical arts, and I have no doubt you would make a fine apprentice, but meanwhile it seems you're needed at home."

The illusionist waited as the laughter died down. "Come now. Is there no one among the fine womenfolk of Memphis brave enough to seek a new life, to test the unknown? Surely among so many lovely ladies, there must be one who thirsts for the knowledge I offer."

"Blasphemer!" came a shout from the back. All heads turned to find a middle-aged man, his face bony and pale as Death's, holding a trembling hand out to point at the Amazing Waldo. The man swung his arms wildly to encompass everyone under the tent. "You're all blasphemers! You turn your faces from the Lord, you worship at the altars of idols, and His punishment on you will be swift and just."

As he spoke, the man advanced through the crowd to stop at the edge of the stage, gesticulating wildly at the people in the audience. "You will be cast down into the fiery pit, where the flames of hell will engulf you, and you will burn without end all through eternity." Breathing like a race horse that has just crossed the finish line, he ended with his arms thrown wide over his head and his eyes turned toward the heavens.

The magician, who had waited until the man stopped speaking, now advanced to the edge of the stage, crouched just to his left, placed a hand on his shoulder, and spoke softly to him. "Brother Jones."

As though startled from his trance, the prophet of doom let his arms fall to his sides and turned to face the conjurer. Never taking his eyes from the man, Waldo stood and pitched his voice loud and strong again for all to hear.

"Brother Jones—this is brother Mordecai Jones, ladies and gentlemen, a man of God who leads the Free Will Baptist Church of the Redeemer's Blood here in your city, I believe. Brother Jones, you need fear no idolatry here." He lifted his eyes to the audience, and the grumbling that had followed the preacher's outburst began to die down. "We are all true believers here, are we not, brothers and sisters?" There were murmurs of assent from the crowd, a few amens and hallelujahs, and at least one "I know that's right."

"As long as I acknowledge and accept that He is the Way and the Light, I don't believe our Lord and Savior doubts my devotion simply because I also respect a knowledge that was ancient when He was born. If you will allow me, Brother Jones, I would be honored to worship with your congregation Sunday morning."

The preacher, whose mouth had fallen open during the illusionist's discourse, nodded dumbly. The Amazing Waldo reached down his hand, the preacher took it, and the magician hauled him up on the stage to stand at his side. He put an arm around Jones.

"Brothers and sisters, in the mystery and glamor that is magic, it is easy to lose sight of what is true and right. Let us thank Brother Jones for reminding us."

At first, the applause was hesitant and sparse. One by one, the illusionist looked the members of the audience straight in the eye until all were applauding vigorously and several had jumped to their feet to wave their arms in the air and a few had danced into the aisles in an ecstasy of devotion. Mordecai Jones, who perhaps had never drawn such a response from his own congregation, blushed crimson.

Waldo released the preacher and stretched out a hand toward the crowd, which fell silent again. The few dancers returned to their seats, and all waited, breathless, to see what would happen next.

"May I join you on Sunday, then, Brother Jones?"

"Glad, uh, glad to have you."

"And all the good people here tonight. Would you welcome them?"

Hands jammed into his pockets, the preacher ducked his head toward the crowd. "Mighty proud to have any and all join us in the Lord's house."

"Thank you, brother!" Waldo clapped him on the back. "You heard him, folks. I hope I'll see many of you at Redeemer's Blood on Sunday. I'll be sitting on the front row."

Jones, who had stood beaming a rictus grin at the Amazing Waldo, now nodded awkwardly out at the audience. The magician put an arm around his shoulders again.

"Brother Jones, I hope you'll be my guest for the rest of the performance. Seems only fair, doesn't it?" The magician motioned to one of the stagehands, who hustled to his side. "Find our friend a seat on the front row, won't you, please? We wouldn't want him to miss anything."

The hand led the bewildered-looking preacher down into the audience to an empty seat that suddenly appeared and ensconced him there.

Joseph Calendar, who knew Waldo worshipped at no altar but that of his own ego, shook his head at the man's temerity.

The Amazing Waldo watched until Jones was settled before he regarded the quiet audience again.

"And now, ladies and gentlemen, I will attempt my most difficult illusion without the aid of an assistant." He flung his cape back from his shoulders and paused dramatically. "Unless, of course, one of you has found the courage to come forward."

In the middle of the crowd, a petite blonde somewhere in her twenties stood and slid past the people seated between her and the center aisle. She hesitated, took one tentative step, then another, and stopped.

"Ah! I believe we have found our fearless volunteer," the Amazing Waldo said. He beckoned her with both hands. "Come forward, my dear, and join me on the stage. Only those who risk all reap life's greatest rewards."

The blonde started forward again.

Unable to watch any further, Calendar slipped from his seat and through the back flap of the tent, where the darkness of the night enfolded him. He would have much to discuss with his guide Imhotep.

Had he not been so deep in thought over the significance of Waldo's appearance and foreboding over what his extended stay might mean, he would have noticed the sturdy figure of a preternaturally tall woman in a hat with a veil pulled over her face who exited the tent hard on his heels. A woman whom the magician's presence had displeased just as much.

Calendar did not note her departure, but the conjurer did. Never one to shrink from a challenge, the Amazing Waldo allowed his lips to quirk up ever so slightly at the corners.

CHAPTER 5

When Calpurnia Waters finally turned up Wednesday morning, she lay crumpled in the alley behind the Odeon Theatre, looking very much like a baby bird that has fallen from the nest, even bonier and more frail than in life.

Knowing Acker was looking for a colored woman who fit the description of the body, Everett Jackson, the homicide detective on duty, had called him when they found her. He and Arnold Acker went way back.

"She's by the alley," he said, directing the sergeant around the side of the theatre.

Dr. Malcolm Mills, the chief medical examiner, had just finished his preliminary scrutiny and signaled for the orderlies to load the body for the morgue, where he would do his utmost to discover what and who had killed her.

"Hang on a second, boys," Acker said. He held a hand up to the ambulance crew, who finished unloading the stretcher and resumed their posts, leaning against the vehicle. "You mind waiting a minute, Jackson?"

The homicide detective jutted his chin toward the body in assent.

"What do you think, Doc?" Acker said.

Dr. Mills stood, peeling off his rubber gloves. "Could have been a lot of things. Her eyes are bloodshot, so suffocation maybe. I don't see any other signs of trauma, but I won't know that for sure until I get her on my table and take a closer look. Rigor has passed, so she's been dead a least a day. Could have been exposure. If she stumbled and fell and was out here in the cold all night. A woman this disabled—a probable polio victim would be my guess—would have had some difficulty getting to her feet with no crutches or braces–"

"No braces?" the sergeant said. "What are you talking about, Doc? Calpurnia Waters walked with canes and wore leg braces."

Crouching beside her again, Dr. Mills grasped one of Calpurnia's feet and turned it for a better look at the side of her shoe. "Well, she is wearing brace shoes, but you can see for yourself there are no braces on her legs. When I examine her, there should be marks that show she wore them, but with these thick cotton stockings, I didn't notice anything here."

Acker flipped through his notes and turned to Brody, the first cop on the scene after the theatre janitor called the police hollering that there was a dead woman out back. "Brody, what did you see when you got here?"

The policeman scratched his chin and thought a minute. "Nothin' but what you're looking at." He pointed at the dead woman. "The body on the ground just like that."

"You didn't move anything? Didn't pick up her cane or any leg braces?"

"This isn't my first dead body, Sergeant."

"What about the janitor? You ask him if he touched anything?"

"He said he didn't." One side of Brody's mouth twitched up. "Scared out of his wits as he was, I believe him. He was shaking when he brought me out back to show me where she was. Said he hadn't ever seen no dead woman before and kept looking over his shoulder like her haint was coming after him. I don't think that fella's going to sleep tonight."

"Mind if I take a closer look, doc?" Acker said.

Dr. Mills stepped back, gesturing to the body. "Go ahead. I've seen everything I need to here."

The sergeant knelt beside Calpurnia, absorbing the position of her body, curled on her side with her arms up over her head like a doll that has been dropped. Gently, he took one tiny claw of a hand in his own. It was as delicate as a child's, but the palms were calloused from years of walking with the canes. He replaced it carefully at her side, resting his own on top of it for a moment. "Damn it," he said under his breath. "Damn it."

He scanned the alley, rose and walked its length and breadth, looking for the missing cane, for anything out of the ordinary. There was nothing but a row of trash cans against the back wall of the theatre. Acker lifted the lid of one. Empty. If Calpurnia had been dead for a day, he couldn't believe no one would have spotted the body. Unless she'd been left there after everyone had departed the theatre for the evening.

"Hey, Brody, ask the janitor when they take the trash out."

"Yes, sir."

Acker returned to Calpurnia's side and stood looking down at her, chewing his lower lip.

After some moments, one of the ambulance drivers shifted impatiently and called out to Acker. "You going to be much longer, Sergeant? We got another call coming in."

"Huh?" Acker started. "No. No, you can go on and take her."

"All right, boys," Dr. Mills said. "Let's get her to the morgue."

The sergeant walked back up the alley, eyes trained on the ground as he went. Even after all these years on the Memphis police force, he couldn't stand watching a body being loaded onto the wagon. It made him think of his father throwing a hog he'd just dipped in boiling water onto the butchering table so he could scrape the hair off the skin. No matter how careful and respectful the attendants were, a body seemed like just so much dead meat once they bagged it and loaded it on the gurney. That was one reason Acker stayed away from homicides when he could help it.

When he heard the ambulance pull away, he found Jackson, who was about to climb into his car and head back to the station. "Mind if I handle talking to the family about this one?"

"Help yourself, Arnold. That's not part of the job that I exactly consider a picnic. "

"Me, either, but I know something about these folks. I'm going to ask the chief to let me give you a hand on this one. That all right with you?"

"Long as you agree to do all the dadgum paperwork." Jackson slapped him on the shoulder. "See you back at the station."

"See you there. I got a couple of stops to make first."

Protocol might dictate that he should go to Calpurnia's house and talk to her mother before he informed Nell Marchand that he had found Hattie's friend, but protocol would have to take a back seat today. He had promised Miss Nell he would let her know the minute he found Calpurnia. Besides, he had a feeling he was going to need back up when he told Hattie she was dead.

CHAPTER 6

It was getting on toward lunch time when Jenkins stuck his head in at the kitchen door.

"Miss Nell," he said. "Sergeant Acker is out front and wants to speak to you. I asked him to wait in the foyer."

Nell and Hattie looked at each other across the kitchen table, where they were shelling the last of the summer peas.

"Why don't you sit here just a minute while I see what the sergeant wants?"

Hattie trained her eyes on the pod in her hand and nodded.

In the front hall, Acker stood with his hat in his hand, studying the checkerboard pattern of the marble floor as though it might divulge some long-sought secret. At the sound of Nell's approaching steps, he looked up. Before he could open his mouth, she knew that the news was not good.

"I'm sorry Miss Nell."

"You've found Calpurnia."

"Yes, ma'am. This morning. Out behind the Odeon. The doc took her down to the morgue."

"Oh, Lord." Nell shut her eyes against the wave of sorrow that swept over her. "All right. Please come on into the kitchen with me, Sergeant. Hattie will want to hear what you've found, and I think it might be a little easier if we tell her together. Would you like a cup of coffee? I think we've still got some from breakfast on the stove, but it might be a little stale."

"Stale or not, I could sure do with a cup."

Hattie did not cry in front of the sergeant. In fact, before the last few days, Nell had never seen her weep since they were children, not even when her mama and daddy had died. But when Nell came into the kitchen after she had shown Sergeant Acker to the door and promised to bring her down to the station, the cook was at the table with her face in her hands, the tears leaking out from between her fingers.

"Oh, Hattie, I'm so sorry." She put her hand on the cook's arm. Hattie stood, collapsed against Nell's shoulder, and began to sob out loud. Nell gasped.

It was dark as pitch and the smell of old wood was just about to make her sneeze. She put out her hands and felt the inside of the mummy case, which was smooth to the touch and strangely warm.

"Hello?" she said. "What do I do now? I'm ready to come out."

Then the floor dropped away under her feet, and she fell onto something soft that cushioned her so that she would make no noise when she landed. Her cane, which had fallen under her, poked her in the back. She gave out a tiny squeak.

"Shhh," a voice said in her ear. "Hush. You have to be quiet or the audience will hear you. Come with me."

"Where are we going?"

"Somewhere safe. Somewhere nothing can hurt you anymore."

That seemed like a funny thing to say, but she rolled onto her knees, doing her best to keep the braces from creaking. A hand grasped hers and pulled her to her feet.

"I left my other cane up there."

"You don't need it now. Take my arm, and I'll help you along. Bend down a little so you don't bump your head on the stage floor. It's not far. Just hold on to me so you don't get lost."

She shuffled forward with the figure that was barely visible next to her, hanging on for dear life.

Then, Nell was back in the kitchen with Hattie holding her at arm's length.

"What did you see?" Hattie said.

NELL PLUNKED DOWN HARD ON ONE OF THE KITCHEN CHAIRS AND blinked at the cook, who crouched beside her, searching her face.

"Someone took her away." Nell forced the words out, still shaking off the effects of her vision. "I couldn't see much."

"He carried Calpurnia off?" Hattie pulled one of the other chairs beside Nell and sat chafing her hands. "You saw a man? Where'd he take her?"

Nell leaned back and closed her eyes. "I don't know. It was just a flash. They were under the stage in the dark." She licked her lips, which were suddenly so dry that they stuck to her teeth. "I need a glass of water, please."

"All right, honey. You want me to fix you some tea?"

"Yes, good and hot. But first the water, please."

"All right. Sit still right here, and get back to yourself. Water and tea coming right up."

Eyes still closed, Nell rested her head against the back of the chair and tried to recall the images. Pinpoints of light fired against her lids, but she couldn't summon Calpurnia's face or even her voice again. The words. She had to remember the words somehow, even though they were already fraying at the edge of her mind. Had the other voice been a man's? She couldn't be sure. These dadgum visions. They did what they wanted, showed what they wanted when they wanted. Her will seemed to have nothing whatsoever to do with them, but what she had seen usually stayed with her longer than this.

Nell dug in the drawer where Hattie kept pencil and paper for shopping lists. She scribbled furiously, the words slipping away almost faster than she could set them down. Joseph would want to know everything she had seen, and it was important to record what she could.

Hattie appeared at her side with the glass of water, set it down silently, and went to the stove to put the kettle on for tea. Nell wrote until she had all the words she could remember down. She gulped at the water, desperate to feel the cool relief of it bathing her throat.

"You want honey and lemon or milk in your tea, Nell?"

"Honey, please, and lots and lots of lemon. I've got this funny taste in my mouth I can't get rid of."

Nell usually took her tea with plenty of milk and sugar, just as her Welsh grandmother, her *nain*, had always liked it. It struck her as odd that Hattie had asked—Hattie who always knew just what she wanted—and odder still that she had wanted the lemon. When the steaming cup was in her hands, the tea was like heaven cutting through the bitter, acrid taste in her mouth and warming her enough to stop the shivering that had made it hard to write.

"All right, then," Hattie said when Nell put down her empty cup. "Can you tell me what you saw?"

"We need Dr. Calendar here. He knows something of the world of illusionists. Even more of it may slip away if I tell it more than once. I want to talk to him before I say anything to anyone else."

Hattie slumped into a chair at the table and buried her face in her hands again. Nell scooted next to her.

"I know you're anxious, but you know we'll do everything we can to find out what happened to Calpurnia. What I saw might not have anything to do with it."

"You know that's not so, Nell."

"No, I can't be sure. It could just be a clue like seeing Ginny Evans and the General together at Bolivar when he'd been dead 40 years before she was born. You should understand more than anyone that I can't control what I see. And I'm only beginning to understand it. I'm sorry, Hattie."

"No. I'm sorry. It's just that the police finding Cal like that, thinking about how she died all alone . . . . It hurts me so I just can hardly stand it."

"We'll find out who did it. With Sergeant Acker and Dr. Calendar on our side, we're bound to."

CHAPTER 7

In her downtown office at the Tabernacle of Light, Sister Louise Henslowe slapped the morning paper down on her desk in the only show of temper her secretary Henry Barcroft had ever witnessed in his 10 years of working with her.

"Record crowds!" she said. "You would think that the disappearance of that poor unfortunate cripple would discourage decent people from attending his performances, but no. Now he's attracting record crowds, and he's extending his engagement. People are nothing but ghouls."

She paused, smoothing her hair and fighting for control. "I'm sorry, Henry. I thought I'd seen the last of that lowdown snake, but now he's here on my doorstep."

"It's not forever, Sister," he said. "The curiosity seekers will tire of him, and he will move on before long. "

"I don't know. He had that audience eating out of his hand. I hear his New York run lasted six months. Six months! And that was without any corpses. But if he's here as much as six days, it's going to feel like eternity. I swear, I could almost believe he turned up in Memphis just to goad me."

"Even the Garden of Eden had its serpent, Sister."

"Yes, and thanks to the serpent, we were all cast out. Vigilance, Henry. Never forget the need for vigilance. If he wants another fight, we'll give it to him. We're going to make the evils of magic the topic of my Sunday radio address. People have to understand just what they're risking. That woman's death is just one instance. I want you to scour the Bible for examples of what happens when we turn to false idols. But remember, gentle exhortation is best. No fire and brimstone."

"Yes, Sister."

CHAPTER 8

The urgency in Nell's voice brought Joseph Calendar to her doorstep within moments after she'd called. Though less so than in the beginning, her visions still unsettled her, he knew, but this time, something had truly frightened her. Perhaps this time, the dreams had been a warning.

Now, in the kitchen with Nell and Hattie, he listened to their stories and thought about how small and fragile Calpurnia appeared as she had stepped into Waldo's mummy case and vanished.

"Hattie, I was in the audience the afternoon your friend disappeared. I confess that like most of the people there, I assumed she was part of the act, that Waldo planned to produce her at a later performance. Had I known she was your friend, that she had truly gone missing, I would have come sooner."

"Joseph, I–," Nell said, looking so stricken that Calendar wished he had considered his words before he spoke. He squeezed her forearm to reassure her.

"I only meant I might have offered support in a time of distress. We don't know what really transpired or if my involvement would have made any difference. Now, Hattie, I want you to tell me everything you can remember of what you saw and heard that afternoon. Then we'll see if Nell can recall her vision. Something in our three perspectives may give us a clue to unravel the mystery."

"Lord, Dr. Calendar, I had no idea you were there," Hattie said. "But it makes sense, knowing what you know and doing what you do."

"Yes, I am a lifelong student of the supernatural, and I've seen Waldo's act before. He is not without certain abilities."

"You ever see him make a person disappear before?"

"Yes, Hattie, I have."

"Did they come back?"

"Most of the time." Calendar glanced at Nell. "But sometimes they didn't reappear until later—much, much later—though."

"But nobody turned up dead."

"Not that I saw, Hattie. Not from his act. I am sorry about what happened to Calpurnia."

"Why would he take her, Dr. Calendar? Why would anybody hurt her? She never did anything to anybody but kindness."

"I don't know. Man is a fallen being, and for some, the temptation to follow the dark path is great. Sometimes we have the misfortune of brushing up against the evil that exists in the world. There is no rhyme or reason to it. Calpurnia had that misfortune. If I'm to be of use, it would help me to know a bit about her. Was she very young when polio struck her?"

"It was our last year of high school. Cal was so beautiful. She was always Miss Everything. We knew she was going to be the homecoming queen, but she got sick not long after we started back to school." Hattie sniffled and wiped her nose on a handkerchief. She swallowed hard a couple of times before she could go on. "Her mama was afraid she might die, and Cal had to go into one of those iron lungs for a while. We didn't know if she would ever come out. But she did. And she learned to walk with canes when nobody ever thought she could. Every time she fell down learning to use those braces, it made me want to cry. But she never complained. Not once."

"She must have been a remarkably brave soul."

"She was. Never been anyone else like Calpurnia." Now, Hattie couldn't go on. She held the handkerchief to her mouth, and tears spilled down her cheeks.

Nell looked to Calendar, her face mirroring the anguish that her friend felt. "Do we have to go on with this now?"

"Intense emotion can clarify memory. I'm sorry, but the more time that passes, the more she may forget. Are you able to continue, Hattie?"

The cook nodded and drew a shuddering breath. "I'm all right."

"Good. Now tell me everything that happened that seemed odd to you during the show."

"Everything about it was crazy. I've never seen a magic show before. Cal was always going on about it, though. One summer, when she went up to Chicago to visit her aunt, they took her to see that Houdini. She couldn't talk about anything else for months. Said there wasn't any kind of chain or trunk Houdini couldn't get out of. Said she'd read how he'd even made an elephant disappear right off the stage in front of everybody. When she heard he was dead, she cried for a week.

"She had this little dog she named Harry after him, and she was always dressing that poor dog up and trying to make him do tricks. I remember one time, she had a jacket on him like something that princess wore in 'The Thief of Baghdad.' Made him a turban to go with it. I think she even tried to make him vanish a time or two."

Hattie smiled at the memory.

"Harry never did learn any tricks, but that dog sat still for all the things she tried to get him to do. Never saw a dog like him for being patient. That's why she wanted to go up there on stage, I guess. That was as close to her own magic show with an audience as she was going to get."

"She sounds quite remarkable," Calendar said.

"First time she saw President Roosevelt on his canes, she said if he could run a whole country being crippled like her, then she didn't have anything to complain about in her job."

"What was her work?"

"Seamstress. She did alterations for Goldsmith. She could take a two-dollar suit and make it look like you spent ten on it. She used to buy remnants down at the fabric store and make the prettiest dresses you ever saw by copying a picture in a magazine. She could just figure out how that dress went together. Cal always looked like she stepped out of a bandbox."

"She doesn't sound like the kind of person who would give up on life despite her difficulties," Calendar said.

"No, sir. Cal never let being crippled get her down. She didn't want any of us feeling sorry for her. I think it hurt her sometimes, especially after she went to see Sister Louise for the healing but didn't come back any different, but she wouldn't let on. Always said that God had given her this trial for a reason, and she had to trust His plan for her." She wiped her eyes. "I can't believe this was it, though—her lying dead out behind the Odeon Theatre like that."

Calendar waited until she composed herself before he spoke again. "Sister Louise?"

"Sister Louise down at the Tabernacle of Light Ministry. Haven't you ever heard her on the radio? She's always carrying on about how she can cure the lame, the halt, and the blind. Claims it's Jesus who does it, but she's His conduit here on earth. Miss Ruby Waters always said hadn't been anybody but Billy Sunday who could tear up preaching on the radio the way Sister Louise does. It was her idea to take Cal down there."

"Of course. Louise Henslowe. She used to have quite an international reputation for miraculous cures. When I was in Vienna, she came through on her tour of Europe."

"Well, the miraculous didn't apply to Cal. After she saw Sister Louise and came back still crippled, she was real quiet for days. Never would tell me what happened, though."

Calendar digested this information and pondered it. "Let's go back to the night Calpurnia disappeared. Was there anything unusual about her that night?"

Hattie thought. "No. She was excited about seeing the Amazing Waldo. Said he was the greatest magician since Houdini. Maybe the greatest ever. Couldn't believe he was coming here to Memphis. Made us buy tickets the day they announced the show in the paper. Got upset because she couldn't get any on the front row."

"Did you talk to anyone at the performance?"

"Who didn't we talk to? We hadn't been in our seats a minute before she was talking to everybody around and finding out all about them and laughing. The little boy next to us wanted to know what was wrong with her, so she told him all about polio and let him stand up with her canes to see what they felt like. Cal never met a stranger. Course, we knew some of the folks sitting around us because she talked about the show all the time. Got our church group interested, and some of them bought tickets, too. Brother Cage was there himself."

"But you didn't notice anyone who seemed to take a particular interest in Calpurnia?"

"No, Dr. Calendar. Nothing like that. People always stared at her like that boy because she had those leg braces, but I didn't see anything else but that."

"All right. Nell, do you feel up to telling me what you saw?"

Nell sighed and pushed her scribbled notes on across the table to him. "Here's everything I could remember. The rest of it is gone. It was so fast that I hardly had time to realize what was happening before the vision ended."

Eyes intense, Calendar read the notes over several times.

"You were obviously experiencing things from Calpurnia's vantage point. I want you to take Hattie's hand, close your eyes, and concentrate. Hattie, you remember as much as you can about that afternoon. Try to let what happened play back through your mind like a movie. Don't try to think or understand, just remember."

They closed their eyes. Nell let her head rest against the back of the chair again.

"Now breathe deeply," Calendar said.

Nell's eyes few open, and she sat bolt upright, snatching her hand from Hattie's.

"No! Stop him," she said, and burst into tears.

"Who, Nell? Stop who?" Calendar said. Her weeping cut though him like a keen wind through silk.

As quickly as they had come, her tears were gone. "Well, goodness."

She scrubbed at her eyes, obviously embarrassed at weeping in front of them and struggling to right herself.

Calendar took her hand, which trembled in his grasp. "Did you see something?"

"Not exactly. I mean, I didn't see it as much as I felt it. Or him." She seemed to struggle to gather her thoughts. "There was a man looming over me in a dark room. I couldn't see his face or anything more than his outline, but I was afraid, so afraid that I couldn't breathe. He spoke to me, but I couldn't make out the words. It was as though they were in another language, a language I felt I should understand. I just knew that his voice dripped menace and that something horrible was about to happen."

She dabbed at her eyes again. "I also knew that the threat was not just for me, that there was someone else. And I knew that I could not stop him alone."

"Did you see or feel Calpurnia?"

Nell closed her eyes briefly. Opened them and shook her head. "No. There was nothing. I didn't see anything of what I saw before. This was something different. Something somehow to do with me." She reached for Hattie's hand. "I'm sorry."

The smile that the cook managed to produce trembled. "You already said it. You can't control what you see. But try to tell Dr. Calendar what you did see about Calpurnia. Maybe if you say it out loud, something will come back."

As Nell recounted what remained of her vision of Calpurnia under the stage, Calendar thought. "This wasn't the same man you sensed just now, then?"

"No. I'm not sure if it was a man with Calpurnia. The voice was so muffled."

"Have you told the police anything?"

"No. We called you first. Do you think we should tell the police?"

"Nell, you told Boss Crump you'd seen Ginny Evans," Hattie said. "I don't think it's going to surprise anybody if you have more visions."

"I don't believe for a minute that Boss Crump has told a living soul that I had vision that persuaded him to go to with us to spring Ginny, especially not the police. He said he received an anonymous tip. You may remember the headlines the next morning claimed he rescued her, and that was fine with me."

"But you can tell Sergeant Acker can't you? That man would walk across burning coals for you if you asked him to."

"I don't know about that, Hattie. There's the beginning of an understanding there that I don't want to ruin. We respect each other, but I don't think I can trust him with news of my psychic powers yet. He seems a little too pragmatic for that."

"Then how you going to explain what you saw? How you going to get him to look under that stage when I already told him I didn't see anything up under there?"

"I know you're frustrated, but we'll find another way. Just what that's going to be, I don't know, but we will."

"What we have to do," Calendar said, "is get the Amazing Waldo to cooperate. He has already revealed the secret of the false floor to Hattie. Perhaps if we remind him that she could, indeed, divulge that secret and spoil one of his favorite illusions, he will be only happy to take the sergeant on his own tour."

"You don't really think anyone else is going to step into that mummy case after what happened to Calpurnia, do you?" Nell said. "I can't believe he'll try it again."

"On the contrary, I believe a frisson of danger will only add to its attraction. Waldo may wait another performance or two just to increase the anticipation, but that case will make its appearance in his act again, and people will line up to step inside. That is human nature."

CHAPTER 9

Louise Henslowe had always insisted on having things her own way. Even as a small child, she commanded the large and loving family of which she was the youngest. Baby, as they called her, had only to look up to have her mother and at least two other attentive siblings waiting anxiously to decipher her wishes and fulfill them. Thus accustomed from an early age to basking in the spotlight, she had come to expect it as her due.

But, now, things decidedly were not going Sister Louise's way. Most decidedly. For the last two Friday evenings, which was when she held her weekly healing gatherings at the Tabernacle of Light Ministry, the audiences had been almost insultingly small. There were hardly enough of the lame, halt, or blind present for her to work any of her miraculous cures. When healings were down, contributions to the Tabernacle were down as well.

And Sister Louise she knew precisely whence the throngs had decamped. They were at the Odeon Theatre watching that fraud who called himself the Amazing Waldo perform his tricks like some ridiculous circus monkey. It was disgusting, really, to have this weekly reminder of the gullibility of the public. Everyone knew there was no such thing as magic, that a man couldn't make anyone or anything vanish, that it was all deceit and deception. Hadn't she proven so before? Souls were the healer's primary concern, of course, not the almighty dollar, but she did have the Tabernacle to maintain, her staff to pay, and more mouths to feed every week. There must be something further that could be done.

Perhaps it was time for an anonymous call to the mayor to complain about the crowds and noise at the Amazing Waldo's shows, to point out the gangs of rowdies who waited to pick the pockets of innocents as they exited, distracted by the so-called wonders they had witnessed.

"Henry," Sister Louise said. There was no sign of her secretary, who usually appeared at her elbow with the same alacrity that had characterized her family. She got up from her desk, crossed to the open door of her office, and peered out. He was not at his usual post just outside. "Henry," she shouted down the hallway.

At that summons, he came at a run from wherever he had been, pushing his wild shock of hair out of his eyes and tucking his checkered shirt into his gray flannel pants. Louise smiled. The boy's sense of style might be somewhat amiss, but he was always poised when it counted, especially when greeting her admiring public or the representative from the radio station that carried her Sunday evening broadcasts. He had an uncanny calm when she herself felt that she might lose hers.

"Yes, ma'am?" he said, sliding to a stop at her door.

"Where were you?"

"Well, I had just stepped down to the—"

"Never mind. What time am I due at the station tomorrow?"

"The same as always, Sister. They need you at 5:30, but if you want, I can call the station and—"

"No, no. Of course . . . 5:30. It slipped my mind somehow, that's all."

"You have more important things to worry about, Sister. That's why you have me, to look after all the little details unworthy of your notice. It is my calling to serve you."

"Yes, Henry, and I do depend on you, perhaps too much sometimes, I think." Sister Louise placed a fond hand on the side of his face. "You're not just my good right arm these days, it seems you're my memory, too. Silly of me to forget such a simple thing. Now, then, do you have my broadcast written?"

"Yes, Sister. Would you like to go over it?"

"Yes. Bring it in, please. I know it will be perfect, but nonetheless, I like to read it through with you." She paused to look back at him over her shoulder. "You really are a paragon, Henry."

"Thank you, Sister. I do what I can."

Resting her hands on the arms of the chair and breathing deeply, Sister Louise sat behind her desk, waiting for her secretary to bring in her radio discourse. She was getting forgetful, but surely it was fatigue and, yes, best to admit it, age. It had lightened her burden remarkably when he had taken over the writing of her radio sermon each week. Now, she could concentrate her powers on her communion with her healing force and her relationship with the Savior, who guided her every step and who had brought her thus far. She sent up a prayer of thanksgiving to Him for Henry, who had turned up at one of her healings ragged, starving, and gibbering about savage nightmares. She had banished his dark dreams, and he had been completely and unquestioningly devoted to her from that moment on.

In entering, the boy was so quiet that she wasn't aware that he had joined her at her desk until he cleared his throat ever so gently to alert her of his presence. He truly was the most thoughtful of assistants.

"Remind me of our topic this week, please, Henry."

"The evils of magic and the folly of those who believe in it."

"Ah, yes, of course. So timely."

He smiled, abashed as though the idea had been his, bless his heart. He passed the papers across the desk to her and waited unobtrusively as she read the discourse. She took a pencil and crossed out the word "Hell" to replace it with "Perdition," but otherwise left the text just as he had composed it. Yes, he had a flair for just the right tone and rhythm to rouse the spirits of her listeners. He understood her so well.

"Excellent, Henry. I think this may be one of your best."

"Thank you, Sister."

"Just be careful about strong language. Billy Sunday may be able to get away with saying Hell out loud in his sermons, but I can't. There are some in my audience who would take exception to a woman's swearing, even if it's not meant as a swear word but an evocation of the Bible's own language. We must remember that many still believe that the fairer sex must be more genteel."

"Yes, ma'am." He blushed. "I'm sorry."

"No, no, there's nothing to apologize for. Just a reminder that not all of our radio congregation are as advanced in their thinking as you and I are. The script is excellent otherwise. There's no need even to retype it. I've substituted just this one word.

Sister Louise put the speech to one side to study later. "Now, how much did we take in last night?"

CHAPTER 10

At Calpurnia's funeral service at the Beale Street Baptist Church, Nell sat on the front pew with Hattie on one side and Joseph Calendar on the other. Calpurnia's brother Leb, who had come down for the service from Chicago, where he worked as a bellman in one of the big hotels, and their mother Ruby sat on the other side of Hattie. Nell had been in the church for funerals before—both Hattie's parents had been buried from there—and for a wedding or two, but she had never before seen the sanctuary so full. The story of what had happened to Cal, of how she had disappeared from the Amazing Waldo's mummy case and turned up dead behind the Odeon Theatre, had gotten out, and there had been a notice in the papers about the funeral. Drawn there by curiosity, probably half the people at the service hadn't known her or ever been to Beale Street Baptist before.

Nell supposed that was all right. Calpurnia deserved a good sendoff, if anybody did.

For the burial afterward in Zion Cemetery, many of the throng of the curious had fallen away. Perhaps the sermon Brother Cage had preached had proven so tame that they were disappointed and chose to move on to their next entertainment or head home for supper with their families. The people gathered under the tent at the graveside to pay their respects were almost all members of Beale Street Baptist. As they approached to express their sympathy to Ruby Waters, Hattie whispered the name and role in the church of each to Nell.

"That's Mrs. Alphonse," Hattie said when a tiny woman with

a commanding presence came up to speak to the family. "She and Miss Ruby been friends a long, long time. Folks always thought her grandson was sweet on Calpurnia and that they would get married one day. He was older, though, and her mama wanted her to wait until we graduated high school. Then Cal got sick, and he married another girl he met working down at the Five and Dime.

"Just about broke Cal's heart. His, too. He never was the same after that. Then, his wife ran off with a railroad conductor. He took to drinking and gambling and staying out all night. Like to worried Mrs. Alphonse to death. Then one night, somebody split his head wide open for cheating at a craps game. Left his grandmama to raise his little brother all by herself. None of that would have happened if he'd married Calpurnia."

Hattie swiped at her eyes with her handkerchief. She had cried off and on all day, and it seemed like every sad story there was to tell came pouring out of her. Her way of grieving, Nell thought. Hattie always put a brave face on everything, and it must all have been pent up in her for too long. Nell, whose own tears were so shallow themselves these days, fished out a clean handkerchief and handed it to her friend, who stuffed the damp one into her purse to join its fellows.

"What in the wide world is he doing here?" Hattie said.

Nell looked up sharply to see the Amazing Waldo kneeling in front of Calpurnia's mother and murmuring something that Nell couldn't quite hear. She shivered, feeling suddenly cold to the bone despite the warmth of the day. She wished for the sweater she had left lying on the bed at home and reached up to clutch at the collar of her dress.

Beside her, she felt Calendar stiffen. He stirred in his seat, moving himself closer to Nell's side.

"Nell, if you are chilly, perhaps we should go and get you out of this raw air," he said in a low voice.

"You are out of your mind if you think I'm about to leave Hattie or get up in the middle of the service. I'm all right."

The words were no sooner out of her mouth than the magician

stood to shake hands with Leb Waters, who had positioned himself beside his mother's chair as the first line of defense in greeting the mourners. Then Waldo turned and looked straight at Nell, a regard that she could have sworn went straight to her soul and stopped her breath in her throat. The feeling that they had met before swept through her, along with an urge to run from the place as fast as her legs could carry her. She had seen his face in newsreels before, and it had been in all the Memphis papers, but Nell was sure that she had never met the man in the flesh. He came to stand as close to her as the range of chairs would allow him and smiled a feral smile at her that bared his canines and did not change the expression of those soulless black eyes with their piercing inquiry. Nell shuddered.

Beside her, Calendar tensed and stirred again as though to rise. She placed a hand on his knee to restrain him, although why she had done so, she could not have said.

"You get your sorry self away from here," Hattie hissed across Nell. "You got a lot of nerve coming here like you were somebody who knew Calpurnia, speaking to her mama like you didn't have anything to do with what happened to her. Wasn't for you and that Egyptian case of yours, Calpurnia would still be here. You get."

The Amazing Waldo switched his gaze to Hattie, who breathed in short, furious gasps and stuck out her chin, daring him to respond. His face seemed to soften slightly, and his eyes took on a normal, human look. It was the face the rest of the world saw. He laced his fingers together in a gesture of supplication and regret and bowed slightly to her.

"My deepest and most sincere apologies," he said, and then he was gone, fading into the crowd of mourners as though he had never been there at all.

Beside her, Nell felt Calendar relax into his chair and heard him let out a breath that he had been holding for an eternity. His face when she turned to him was pale and cold as marble, his eyes fixed on the spot where the magician had disappeared.

CHAPTER 11

Across town in an area that had once been perfectly acceptable for those of modest means, Mordecai Jones consulted his Bible and wondered if he had chosen the subject of his next morning's sermon wisely. If, as he had promised in front of the audience the Sunday evening before, the Amazing Waldo did appear at Redeemer's Blood for Sunday morning service and if members of said audience attended as he had invited them to, Brother Jones wanted to be at his very best.

The topic of his text had cost him several sleepless nights, but he hoped he had hit on just the right theme in choosing Isaiah 64:6 to remind them that they were all sinners. He might never again have the opportunity to address a gathering as large as the one he anticipated, to reach so many sinners and guide them to the way. It might be his chance to make his mark at last after so many years of slaving away in tiny, out-of-the-way churches. He wasn't some jake-leg you tossed a nickel to when you passed him hollering about salvation on a street corner. They would all finally recognize him for what he was, the Lord's own true disciple.

Jones went to his small closet and pulled out his severe black Sunday suit. The fabric had worn shiny in places like the elbows and knees and the front about halfway up, where he liked to tug at it when he was really getting going good about the Lord's mercy. If tomorrow's collection turned out to be good, he might—might, not would—buy himself a new suit. Meanwhile, he ran the brush over the old one to make sure there was not so much as a speck of lint. One of his more-devoted parishioners had laundered it for him on her Wednesday wash day, so it was fresh.

One day, he would dress himself in robes like Sister Louise Henslowe, but not in white. No, he would choose black as a stern reminder that the Devil was at hand and that darkness, not the Light, was the way that the Devil chose. They would set off his pallid skin, skin pale as some girl's, his daddy used to say. But like Sister Louise, he would emblazon his robes with a crimson cross. Crimson for the blood of the Lamb to remind his congregation that His blood had been shed for them on that cross to redeem their sins, the blood after which he had named his church. Yes, black robes for him but maybe red for the choir he would have singing behind him each service. Folks remembered red.

Next, he unwrapped the sparkling white new shirt he had gone all the way downtown to Lowenstein's to buy for Sunday's service. He'd also had a haircut and shoeshine, reassuring himself that they were not vanities but part of the Lord's work.

His clothes and shoes arranged to his liking, Jones knelt at his bedside and asked the Lord to guide him along the important road ahead.

CHAPTER 12

Back at the Marchand house after the afternoon's services, Hattie bustled around the kitchen getting their supper together, muttering all the while to Nell and Joseph Calendar but mostly to herself.

"That low-down, big-mouthed so-and-so had no business showing up at Calpurnia's funeral like that," she said. "I should have gotten up out of my chair and smacked him into the middle of next week. Only reason I didn't is because I didn't want to carry on in front of Miss Ruby like that, especially not today. He already made enough of a scene just by being there. I don't think Cal's mama and Leb realized just who he was, thank goodness, or I bet Leb would have cleaned his plow."

They had all eaten at the wake at the Waters house, but that didn't keep the cook from setting out half a country ham that she had baked the day before and putting a pot of greens on the stove to cook with some of the ham hock. She pulled her apron on over her black funeral dress, rolled up her sleeves, and started a batch of biscuits.

"At least he had the decency not to come to the Waters's house afterward, Hattie," Nell said, picking at the ham and popping a bite into her mouth.

"Now, I know I could not have held back if he had. I would have grabbed him by the neck and thrown him right out the door, and I bet he knew it. Sorry so-and-so."

"He's certainly peculiar. The way he looked at me made me feel as though I didn't have any clothes on." She shivered again at the memory.

Calendar, who had not spoken since the graveside, turned to her. "Are you quite recovered?"

"Yes. Of course. It was just odd, is all. He acted as though he knew me, although how he could is beyond me. I tell you one thing, even if I had ever had any desire to go down and see his performance, nothing could make me do it now."

"You haven't got any business traipsing down there anyway, Nell." Hattie paused long enough to slide the pan of biscuits into the oven and wash the flour off her hands at the sink. "Man isn't anything but a snake. A lowdown snake. Isn't that right, Dr. Calendar?"

When he didn't answer right away, both women glanced over at the medium.

"The Amazing Waldo is not someone to be taken lightly. He has a reputation for being quite ruthless under certain circumstances."

"You know him?" Nell said.

"Our paths have crossed." Calendar reached for a nibble of ham himself. "Hattie, how did you know I've been dreaming about your ham and biscuits?" he said, a deflection from the topic of the illusionist that was not lost on Nell. "What will Mrs. Waters do now that Calpurnia has been laid to rest? Seems to me that house could be much too lonely for one person."

"She's going up to Chicago with Leb. He's got six children, and she says they need her up there. I guess she would have moved a long time ago if she hadn't felt like she couldn't go off and leave Cal all on her own. Leb wanted both of them up there, but Cal wouldn't go. Said she was born in Memphis, and she wasn't studying on being anywhere else. She wanted to be buried by her daddy some day." Hattie sniffed and blotted at her nose with her handkerchief. "Well, I guess she got her wish."

"What will happen to the house?" Nell said.

"Leb says he's going to sell it. His mama doesn't want to live in it anymore, and he's sure not planning on coming back to Memphis any time soon. Says Chicago has too many opportunities. His wife is from up there, you know. All those children been born in Chicago, too. They wouldn't have the first idea about what to do in Memphis, Tennessee. I guess it was bound to happen once Miss Ruby's sister went up there."

Hattie took down three plain white dinner plates and set them on the counter.

"Mrs. Alphonse is sure going to miss her, though. She and Miss Ruby have been singing in the choir together long as anybody can remember."

"Have you ever thought about leaving Memphis, Hattie?" Calendar said.

"No, sir. Only way I'm going anywhere is if Nell takes it into her head to run off somewhere like New York or Paris. She went to Paris without me that one time, but if she figures on going again, she's got to take me with her."

"You know I'm not going anywhere without you," Nell said. "But what if you decide to get married and your husband wants to take you off to some other town?"

"Huh. No way I'm going to marry a man who thinks he's going to make me go somewhere I don't want to go. Besides, I got too much to do running the house and looking after you, Miss Bess, and Mr. Jenkins to think about a man. Unless you decide you need a good-looking butler like that Simon who works with Dr. Calendar. We could use another hand around here."

"A butler?" Nell said. "Hattie, I don't think we're nearly as fancy as Dr. Calendar. We've got Jenkins anyway."

"What about you, Dr. Calendar?" Hattie said. "If you couldn't live in Memphis, where would you go?"

Calendar thought a moment. "I'm with you, Hattie. I'm staying right here unless Miss Nell goes somewhere else. But if I had to leave Memphis, I would go back to Vienna. It's a beautiful, cultured place filled with educated people. Not now, of course, with all the trouble Adolf Hitler and the Germans are stirring up in Europe, but some day when the world settles down again. I hope they don't destroy it.

"After Vienna, I would have to say New York. It's so alive. The theatre. The museums. The food. There's no other city in the world that compares with it. But there's also nowhere else in the world I can get biscuits like yours, Hattie. Don't you think those are about done?"

"I believe they are. Now, y'all carry these dishes and the ham on into the dining room. I'll be along in a minute with the biscuits."

CHAPTER 13

As Brother Mordecai Jones had hoped, Sunday morning service at the Church of the Redeemer's Blood was packed to the rafters. Worshippers of all races and creeds had always been welcome in his house, but he had never seen as many coloreds in the congregation as there were today. They crowded the back pews. All the churches down on Beale Street must be just about empty this morning. Brother Jones hoped their pockets were as deep as their curiosity. He could almost feel those fine new black robes settling across his shoulders.

He peered out over the congregation, looking for the Amazing Waldo among them. He spotted the magician on the front row near the aisle, where he had promised to be, wearing a gray suit, a crisp white shirt, and a red tie. He looked like a million bucks, like a Rockefeller.

The preacher ran an absent hand over his hair and tugged at the hem of his own jacket. One day, he'd have made-to-order suits just like that. It couldn't hurt to dress well as he carried out the Lord's work. Everybody could see he was a humble man, a man unashamed of the poor country people he had come from. Folks said Billy Sunday had the common touch, and that was part of what had made the evangelist so effective. Mordecai Jones stopped short of running across the sanctuary and sliding to stop at the base of the cross like he was sliding home, but a little showmanship like Sunday's wasn't a bad thing. Look at how folks had eaten up every fancy trick the Amazing Waldo dished out.

Sister Florence had finished banging out "At the Cross" on the piano, and the last notes of the choir were dying away when Brother

Jones stepped into the pulpit. He looked out over the congregation, waiting for the gossiping and fussing to die down. When the last talkative old biddy had closed her mouth and the last fidgety child had stopped kicking the back of the seat in front of him, Jones opened his Bible. Every eye in the house was trained on him, and it was so quiet that you could have heard a gnat fart.

The preacher cast a glance over his shoulder at the cross. *Lord, speak through me.* He turned back toward the congregation, closed his eyes for a moment to collect his thoughts, and drew in a deep breath. "Brethren, today's lesson comes from the Book of Isaiah Chapter 64, Verse 6. 'But we are all as an unclean thing, and all our righteousnesses are as filthy rags; and we all do fade as a leaf; and our iniquities, like the wind, have taken us away.'"

The scripture reading complete, he closed his Bible and stepped away from the pulpit to stand at the center of the altar. He had never preached like this before, but this was a day of new beginnings. "Brothers and sisters," he said, his voice ringing out over the congregation true and strong, "As Isaiah tells us, we are all sinners. But today, I want you to think not of a God of vengeance, not of a God of judgment who weighs your heart on His heavenly scale against your sins and decides whether you will be cast down into the fiery pit or lifted up with be with Him and his angels in paradise.

"No, brethren, this morning, I want you to think about a loving and forgiving God, a God who holds out his arms to each of you and pulls you into His embrace." Jones spread his arms wide over the congregation and the hugged them to himself to demonstrate how the Lord would clasp a sinner to his bosom. "I want you to think of God as our Father who loves us."

Half an hour later, Brother Mordecai Jones ended his sermon in his shirtsleeves, drenched in sweat from the fervor of his exhortation but exalted. He stopped again at the center of the altar, reaching toward Heaven, turning his eyes in the same direction, and shouting "Hallelujah!" Slowly, he lowered his arms until he stretched his palms toward the congregation. He emerged from his ecstasy to look at them and saw that many were crying clean out loud without caring a bit who saw them. They were ready for the Call.

"Now, brothers and sisters, if you have felt the hand of the Savior reach out to touch your heart, if you are ready to acknowledge God's love, if you are ready to accept the Lord Jesus Christ as your savior and redeem yourselves from sin in His precious blood, then come forward now. Come to the altar and lay your soul at the foot of the cross. Dedicate your life in service and worship to Him."

Mordecai Jones waited, but at first no one moved. It was as though they were frozen, mesmerized. His heart, which had been lifted up so high, began to sink. Why didn't they come? He was about to repeat his invitation when the Amazing Waldo, the magician himself, stepped out into the aisle and came to kneel at the altar. "Hallelujah, brother!" Jones shouted, resting a hand atop Waldo's head. "Hallelujah!"

And then they came in droves, jostling each other in their urgent rush forward. Men and women came. Colored and white. Grandfathers. Young mothers with babies in arm and their other children in tow. They came to accept the Lord. Brother Jones knelt to pray and lay his hands on each one. It took him more than an hour to speak with them all. It was the greatest moment of his life.

———

JOSEPH CALENDAR WAS ALSO AMONG THE CONGREGATION FOR BROTHER Jones's sermon at the Church of the Redeemer's Blood. He did not join the throng at the altar, but he thought very carefully about what purpose Waldo could have had in coming forward. He knew for a fact that the magician was no Christian. It would be worthwhile to see how the news spread and how Waldo would use it to his advantage.

CHAPTER 14

In the kitchen beneath the sanctuary of the Tabernacle of Light, Sister Louise stood as she did every weekday evening, handing out loaves of bread to the poor who had gathered to be fed, Henry at her side to hold the basket. Evelina Milam, the stage manager, poured a glass of milk for each. No matter how far she traveled or how famous she became, Louise had promised herself that she was not above such humble work, that just as Jesus had fed the multitude, it was her calling to do so as well and to speak with each soul who came to her for spiritual and physical sustenance. So many of the destitute now came each day to be fed that she knew them by name.

An especially careworn woman wearing the tatters of what once must have been a decent if simple dress made her way through the line. At her side was a teenage boy dressed neatly in worn overalls and work shirt whom Louise guessed must be her son. What little the woman had, she obviously gave to him.

"Thank you, Sister Louise," the woman said, unable to meet her eye.

Louise took the woman's hand as she pressed the loaf into it. "I don't recognize you, sister. Have you been with us before?"

Startled, the woman looked up, dismay washing over her face and pulling the corners of her mouth down even further. "No, ma'am, but . . . but we heard down at the bus station that you were feeding folks here, and we thought it would be all right. Please, at least let my boy have something. I'm not really hungry anyway."

"Of course, it's all right." Louise took in the woman's gaunt cheeks and sunken eyes and felt the bird bones that stood out in the hand she held. "You are both welcome to be fed with us. I would like to offer you solace for your soul as well as bread for your body. Tell me about your troubles."

The woman trembled as relief replaced apprehension. "Yes, ma'am. In the drought over in Arkansas two years back, we lost our farm. The sheriff and the fella from the bank who held our note came to turn us out, and my man shot himself in the barn. Blamed himself for what happened to us. The boy and I been walking ever since, stopping wherever we could find work. We heard there might be jobs in factories in Memphis, so we came here."

"Do you have a place to stay?"

"No, ma'am. We don't have anything but the clothes we're standing in."

"Evelina."

The stage manager handed her pitcher to a woman pouring coffee beside her.

"Yes, Sister Louise?"

"Find this lady and her son a quiet corner to eat their meal. When they have finished, take them over to the mission house and see if they can't find beds for them."

"Yes, Sister."

"You will always be welcome at the Tabernacle," Louise said to the woman and boy. She nodded to Evelina.

"Bless you, Sister," the woman said, and kissed her hand. Evelina led them away.

"I'd like to see that magician and his preacher pawn do that," Henry said.

"The Lord sent that mother and her child to us, Henry," Louise said. "There are many we cannot save, but pray that He always gives us the means to help the truly desperate."

CHAPTER 15

Down by the Illinois Central rail yard on Iowa Avenue, the sun was beginning to slant toward the horizon. J.C. Alphonse took the bandana out of his back pocket to wipe the sweat from his face.

"Hey, dummy!"

The foreman stood right in front of J. C.'s face and hollered. J.C. could tell he was hollering because his skin went all red and his eyes bugged out the way people's did when they were mad. Seemed like the foreman was always mad at him for this thing or that. It had taken him a while to understand that J.C. couldn't hear anything he said, no matter how loud he said it. Couldn't hear anything, for that matter, not even the Last Trump on Judgment Day if it came. Now he mostly remembered to get around where J.C. could read his lips.

"Hey, dummy," he repeated. "You didn't bring me that bucket of bolts like I told you."

J. C. nodded and pointed to the bucket by the pile of lumber the foreman had himself been sitting on when he had ordered the bolts.

The foreman slapped his pointing finger down and got back in J.C.'s face. "Fetch it here, boy."

J.C. hauled the bucket over and set it carefully at the foreman's feet. The man picked up the bolts, turned to the group working on framing the warehouse they were building, and started yelling at someone else, waving his arms around like a scarecrow in a high wind. He was almost always hollering at somebody about something.

Dummy. J.C. hated it when people called him dummy. He

especially hated it when the foreman called him that. He hated it when some of the other men on the crew stood just far enough away that he couldn't read their lips and said things to him that he couldn't hear and then laughed because he couldn't understand. But he needed the job, so he took it the way he would probably have to take it from now until Kingdom Come.

He wasn't a dummy, his Grandmama Alphonse had told him over and over. He just couldn't talk like other folks because he couldn't hear what the words were supposed to sound like. Hadn't she taught him how to read and write? She always said if Helen Keller could learn to read and write even blind like she was, he should be able to, too, because there wasn't a thing in the world wrong with his eyes. Some of the white men working on the crew couldn't even write their names. He knew because they signed with X's when they picked up their money on payday.

J. C. was busy nailing a crossbeam to a door jamb when he felt a tap on his shoulder. He looked around, and one of the other carpenters grinned at him and pointed at his watch. Quittin' time! He grinned back at the man, his only friend on the crew, and nodded. He needed to get home quick, get his chores done, and wash up before supper. Then he and his grandmama were going to see the magic show one of the ladies she cleaned house for had given her tickets to.

"Come on in here, baby, and get you a cool drink," his grandmother said when he brought his lunch pail into the kitchen for her. She hugged him. "I know you must be worn clean jab out after swinging that hammer all day. Get you a cool drink and go get ready. We got smothered pork chops and collards for supper. And cornbread. Grandmama's going to fix you a nice, hot skillet of cornbread to have with your supper. Sound good?"

J.C. nodded and kissed her on the cheek. It was their nightly ritual. She told him what they were having for supper, talking to him just like he could hear but keeping her face turned to him so he could read what she was saying. When they found out he was deaf, some people exaggerated their words as though that could make him hear better. All it did, though, was make their mouths all funny so he couldn't understand a single word. But Grandmama, she always treated him like he was just like everybody else.

"You want a real bath tonight before the magic show? I got the kettle on, and I can fill the tub for you."

He smiled.

"All right, then, baby. I'll have that water ready for you in no time. You go get your work boots off. Got your clean clothes laid out on the bed."

Scrubbed and fresh and well fed on Grandmama's pork chops and greens, J.C. slid onto the front seat of her Model T beside her. She slipped it into gear and eased away from the curb. Sometimes when there wasn't too much traffic, she let him drive even though he didn't have a license. She said that one day when she was gone, he'd have to know how, so he might as well learn by doing now. He didn't like to think what his life would be like when she wasn't around to look after him.

"Don't you fret yourself one minute about that, J.C.," she always said. "Fine, good-looking boy like you, there's plenty of girls are going to want you. You're not going to be all by yourself when I go on to Glory, which isn't going to be for a good, long time anyway, so don't you worry about that."

Because his grandmother always liked to arrive early, they found a good parking place on the street close to the Odeon Theatre where they were having the magic show now. J. C. would like to have seen it while it was under the big tent. His grandmother had taken him to the circus once under a tent, and he had loved the elephants. But he was glad to see the show at all, wherever they had it and even without elephants.

Walking up to the theatre, they saw a placard that read "The Amazing Waldo" under a picture of the magician holding up a dove. Below it was a smaller photo of a pretty blonde girl in tights standing next to some kind of tall box with funny writing and a man's face on it.

The caption under it read, "and featuring his lovely assistant Penelope, Memphis's own magical mystery."

They stopped at the concession stand to buy a cold bottle of Coke to share and some peanuts. These weren't in the shells the way Grandmama roasted them at home but in a bag already picked out and salted. They settled in their seats on the front row of the colored section. J.C. had never been so close to a stage before. The lights were dazzling, and there was a smell like the soap his grandmother put on her floors when she scrubbed them. The tall box from the picture on the sign out front stood in the middle of the stage.

The lovely assistant Penelope came out first, bringing a covered tray that she set on a table by the box. She walked to the edge of the stage right in front of them and said, "Ladies and gentlemen." She stopped, watching the audience with a patient look. "Ladies and gentlemen, it is my great pleasure to introduce to you the Amazing Waldo."

The magician sauntered out from behind the curtain and stood by Penelope. He bowed, swirled the cape he wore over his shoulders, and kissed her hand.

"Good people of Memphis, in honor of your own Penelope, tonight we will attempt an illusion never before tried on these shores. Not successfully, that is. It is an ancient ritual once used by the priests of Egypt to call down great power for their pharaohs. Its secrets have passed to me though channels I am sworn never to disclose. Should our illusion fail, the spirits I am about to invoke will be angry, and we will all be in very grave danger, so if some among you are faint of heart and wish to leave this place before I undertake it, now is the time to do so."

The people around them nudged and jostled each other, but no one got up from their seats.

Then the Amazing Waldo moved to the other side of the stage, and J.C. could no longer see what he was saying. Penelope walked back and forth, holding two funny curved swords over her head. She handed them to the magician, who waved them in the air and said something to the audience.

In the seat next to him, Grandmama turned to look back at the crowd behind them, so J. C. did, too. There was a big old red-faced man in the middle of the white section hollering and pointing at the stage. J.C. couldn't tell what he was saying, but the magician answered him. More hollering and then another answer from the stage before the man made his way to the aisle and past their seats to the stage.

J.C. sucked in his breath. It was the foreman from work. Penelope took the man by the arm and had him lie down on some kind of bed that they had brought out next to the big box when he wasn't looking. Then she put a dark blue blanket with a pattern of suns and moons over him until she covered everything up but his head.

The Amazing Waldo came back to the edge of the stage and waved the swords around some more, talking for what seemed to J. C. like forever. Then he got behind the bed and handed one of the swords to his assistant. He said something to the foreman, and the foreman answered back before the magician raised the sword he still had in his hands as far up as he could reach and then brought it down—flash!— onto the foreman's neck. The man's head fell clean off and into a basket they had under it.

J. C. jumped up and screamed again and again. His grandmother tried to get him to stop, but he couldn't. He screamed until there was no air left in his lungs, and then he dropped down on the ground in front of his seat. He had time to look up and see Grandmama's face over him, looking worried, before he passed out.

THERE WAS A FAINTER IN EVERY CROWD. EVERY TIME HE PERFORMED the decapitation trick, at least one member of the audience fainted and had to be carried out. But he'd never before heard the kind of ear-splitting cry that the Negro boy in the front row let out, the boy who had stared so intently at him every time he caught his eye. It was a cry more like an animal in its last agony than anything he'd ever heard come out of the mouth of a human being before. It was like a soul being cast down into the fires of Hell for eternal torment.

And this time, it totally spoiled the illusion. His subject, the beefy, florid man he'd enticed from the audience before whispering the secret of the trick in his ear and securing his agreement to go along for a nice little sum, jumped to his feet at the sound and ran to the edge of the stage to peer down at the fallen boy.

"Well, I'll be dadgum," the subject said. "It's the dummy." He jumped off the stage to join the crowd that was gathering around the prone form and that the old woman with the boy was trying vainly to hold back.

"Y'all get on back," the beefy man said, waving an arm at them. "This is one of my boys works for me. You need to give him some air." When the crowd failed to do as he had bid them, the man gathered the unconscious boy in his arms and lifted him as gently to the stage as if he'd been a newborn.

Waldo knelt beside him and took one of the boy's hands. "It's all right. Everything is all right. It's safe to wake up now."

"It itn't no use talking to the dummy," the red-faced man called up. "He's stone deaf. Can't hear nothin'."

"His name's J. C.," the old woman who had been with the boy said to him. "Don't you go calling my grandson dummy."

The florid man had the good grace to look deflated at that.

She reached up her hands and Waldo lifted her up onto the stage, too. She knelt beside her grandson and stroked the side of his face. "All right, baby, it's time to wake up."

The boy's eyelids fluttered and then opened. He stared around him in terror until she took his face in her hands. "It's all right, J. C. The man wasn't hurt. See, he's standing right there." She pointed, and the boy's gaze followed until he saw him and sat up with a smile of such unmistakable relief and joy that even the red-faced man saw and must have understood it for what it was.

"Your grandmama's right, boy," the man said. "I ain't hurt."

J.C. then turned to Waldo, wide-eyed. The magician leaned down to be sure he could see his lips. "It was an illusion, son, a misdirection to make people believe that they're seeing something that they're not. After the show, if you come back stage, I can show you how it works."

The boy sat up and nodded.

"You all right now, baby?" the old woman said.

He nodded again and got to his feet.

"Want to go on home?"

He shook his head violently.

"Want to stay for the rest of the show?"

He grinned at her.

"All right. We'll stay." She patted his hand before turning to Waldo. "You going to cut any more heads off tonight?"

"No," the magician said. "That was my quota for the evening. I promise there will be no more bloodshed."

She nodded as though to tell him there'd better not be. She put her arm through the boy's, and he led her back down to their seats.

"Ladies and gentlemen," Waldo said, "if you will all return to your seats, we will go on with the show."

Still muttering, the people who had gathered around J. C. made their way back to rejoin the audience. Waldo saw a dark figure move toward the back, but this time, he paid it no heed.

CHAPTER 16

Backstage after the performance, Waldo wondered again about the striking red-haired woman with Joseph Calendar at the funeral, on whom his thoughts had lingered from the moment he spotted her sitting next to his old nemesis. He had heard that Calendar was in Memphis practicing as a medium, but was the woman at the graveside with his enemy the one Waldo sought?

When their eyes met at the cemetery, he had felt a stirring of something familiar about her. Calendar's reaction when he saw Waldo had told him that whoever she was, she mattered to him. The magician had been reaching into her soul for the spark that would tell him he had found her when the Negress at her side, the one who had bedeviled him so after her friend vanished from his case, had interrupted him.

There was time to find out who Calendar's companion was. As long as the Amazing Waldo could pack the house for each performance, he was content to stay in Memphis for a while. That unfortunate cripple's death had brought him notoriety that filled the theatre night after night. And tonight's incident with the deaf boy, well, he could not have planned it better himself. More dignified presentations might better suit his tastes, but if chaos filled his coffers, so be it.

Calendar would be an impediment, but Waldo would not let that deter him. They had last crossed horns in Vienna, where it had ended badly for all of them—Calendar, Waldo, and the girl Sarah. A pity, really, because that one had been particularly beautiful. He had intended only to free her from Calendar's influence and draw her into

65

his own, to plant the seed with her family that her work as a medium was not appropriate for a girl of her station in life. How was he to know that they would send her to Sigmund Freud to cure her of her visions and that his treatments would drive her mad?

Even if they could somehow expunge their ancient enmity, for what had happened to the beautiful Sarah, Calendar would never forgive him. Waldo believed it was the medium himself who had found her body shattered on the pavement beside St. Stephens, the urgent, inescapable voices that screamed more shrilly in her head each day finally stilled. Freud should have understood she was in an impossible position, forced to choose between her family who insisted that she abandon her gift and the voices that would give her no peace. It had been a terrible waste.

Perhaps he and Calendar had both been wrong and Sarah had not been their lost love. And if she was, who was this Memphis woman of whom Calendar was so protective? She was a beauty, too. Had that beauty been enough to move Calendar to love again?

Perhaps he could win her away from his old enemy simply for the sport of it. There would be less of the triumph and revenge he craved in taking her, but anything that caused Joseph Calendar pain was to the good by Waldo's thinking. Until the day that Tadinanefer was his and the battle they had fought over the centuries ended, Waldo could only hope to cause him as much suffering as possible. The subtler the undertaking, the better.

Waldo searched for his walking stick, which Matilda had always known to place by his coat along with his watch and fob. Time, he liked to say, stood still when he was on the stage. It had no meaning for him, no use, until he reentered the world of the mundane.

He had yet to decide whether the new girl Penelope was simply too stupid or too lazy to learn his preferences. She couldn't tell the difference between the gin and the vermouth, his shirts came back with so much starch that they crackled when he forced his arms into the sleeves, and she never called poor Sekhmet by the right name, which was most distressing for the sensitive creature. But perhaps it was his fault. He should never have chosen a girl who had grown up with servants of her own.

With Matilda, who had been so eager to serve his every need for so long, he had fallen into the habit of having his assistant assume the role that his manservant-secretaries had always played before. His assistants had been ornaments and amusements, and the men he employed had taken care of the business, arranged his travel, and known how he liked his shirt collars pressed.

Matilda had rendered a manservant superfluous. When Hubert, his last, had grown too decrepit to look after him properly, she had suggested that Waldo could save the not-inconsiderable fee he had paid his loyal retainer by allowing her to take over his duties. So, Waldo had packed the old man off to Burgundy to a comfortable retirement in the house of his son and frugal daughter-in-law.

What a pity she had decided that she wanted more. That she, in fact, wanted to become Mrs. Waldo Peterfreund, settle them down somewhere as safe and predictable as Sandusky had been, and raise a passel of little Peterfreunds to look after them in their dotage. Waldo had had a certain affection for her, and she warmed his bed on many a cold night in the most satisfactory manner, but a wife and family had never been part of his plan. Would never be. He hoped Matilda found what she was looking for back in Chicago. She deserved a house full of children and a husband who spoiled her. Those were not things that the Amazing Waldo would ever be able to give any woman but one, not in this life or any of those to come.

"Penelope, my dear," he called out. "Do you know what you've done with my walking stick?" He slipped the watch and fob into his pocket.

"I'm sorry, Waldo," the girl said, hurrying to his side with it in her hand. "I don't know why I can't remember."

"It's all right, dear girl. Now, shall we dine in tonight, or would you rather go out?"

"Out," she said.

"I suspected as much. Now put on your coat, we'll go back to the suite and dress to the nines, and I'll call for a car."

She bounced away, and he couldn't help an indulgent smile. She was, after all, hardly more than a child. With time and patience, she would learn his likes and dislikes. Meanwhile, he would look into hiring a manservant. He could wire the venerable agency he preferred working with in New York, the people who had provided the very satisfactory Hubert for him. He could certainly afford someone, and if Penelope continued as scatterbrained as she had so far proven to be, then it would preserve the peace between them to have someone else he could depend on.

CHAPTER 17

It sure was gloomy down here by the river in the evening. J. C. wished more than once that the boss had sent somebody else to deliver the load of bricks to the warehouse past the docks where the steamboats came in. He about knew he'd made him do it because J. C. couldn't complain about it. Part of him guessed he ought to be glad the boss trusted him to drive the company truck.

"You know you the best man he got on his team, J. C.," his grandmama said when he wrote out that he would be late for supper because he had to drive a load of bricks after work. "Course, if he'd thought about it, he should have sent you during the daytime, but I guess he just wants to get an extra hour or two out of you. But don't you worry, baby. I'll have your supper hot for you when you get home."

J. C. found the address on the piece of paper the foreman had given him and pulled the truck up as close to the loading dock of the rundown old warehouse as he could get. There wasn't a soul in sight, and since J. C. couldn't holler to let them know he was there, he climbed down off the truck to knock on the door. First touch of his knuckles, and it swung open. He stepped inside but still didn't see anybody.

He was just about to turn around and drive those bricks back to the yard when he spied a piece of paper lying on the ground over to the side of the door. He picked it up and saw that it was a note that must have been pinned to the door and fallen off when it opened. It read, "Unload bricks around back. Use wheelbarrow."

His grandmama taught him never to shirk his responsibilities, but J. C. couldn't help wishing he could get on home to his supper. Dutifully, he closed the door, fired up the truck, and headed around to the back of the building, where it was even darker than it had been out front. If he left his headlights on, he could see just well enough to unload the bricks in the red wheelbarrow he found overturned against the wall.

"Sooner you get started, sooner you'll finish," his grandmama always told him. "Any time you got a disagreeable job to do, just do it and get it over with. No use in spending your time dreading it. That just makes it worse."

"Yes, ma'am," he thought in response.

J. C. had just stacked the final brick in the last pile and put the wheelbarrow back against the wall where he'd found it when he felt something brush against his sleeve that made him just about jump out of his skin. People were always sneaking up on him, thinking it was funny when he flinched because he couldn't hear them coming.

He swung around to see who it was, but before he could spy anybody, some kind of bag came down over his head and shoulders, pinning his arms to his sides. J. C. struggled, but the bag was so tight that he couldn't move his arms. Whoever it was grabbed him and pushed him. He tried to dig in his heels, but without his arms to balance himself, he had to stumble in the direction he was pushed.

Something banged against the middle of his thighs that he thought must be the tailgate of his truck. His attacker spun him and shoved him backward so that he fell into the truck bed and lay there on his back like an old box turtle in the middle of a country road. He felt a shudder that had to be somebody closing the tailgate. For a moment, he wallowed around trying to right himself until he realized he couldn't and lay still, panting.

Then, he felt the vibration of the truck engine starting up. Whoever was behind the wheel slammed the truck into reverse, slinging J. C. against the cab, and then floored it so that he hit the tailgate hard. Deaf and blinded now, all he could sense was the shimmy of the vehicle as it made its way through the Memphis streets, taking him he didn't know where.

J. C. wondered if he would ever see his grandmama again and began to cry.

He wasn't sure how long they drove along like that before the truck stopped. He felt the tailgate slam open, and hands grabbed him by the ankles to drag him out. At least whoever it was let him sit up and rolled him out to his feet instead of pulling him so that his head hit the tailgate on the way down. The hands steadied him, turned him. One went to the small of his back, urging him forward. When he stumbled, his captor grabbed him by the elbow to steady him and let him slow down enough to feel his way with his feet.

They passed through a doorway. J. C. could tell because he tripped on the threshold when one toe hit it. The hands steadied him again. They came into a room with a light overhead that he could just make out through the burlap of the bag. The hands backed him against a chair and pushed him hard enough to make him sit down.

Then the bag came off, and J. C. had just enough time to see the face that stared down at him not unkindly before the lights went out and J. C. screamed a scream that he could not hear.

CHAPTER 18

The elderly Negro woman who made her way to the police station early Friday morning was so diminutive that the sergeant on duty had to lean over the front desk a little to see her.

"Something I can do for you?" he said.

"I'm here about my grandson. He didn't come home from work last night."

"You sure he wasn't just out tying one on with some of his friends and couldn't make it home? You know, getting an early start on the weekend."

"No, sir," she said, drawing herself up to her full height. "I didn't raise that kind of boy. My J. C. doesn't drink. He knows liquor killed his daddy and his brother, and he promised me a long time ago that he wasn't ever going to touch it."

The sergeant leaned his forearms against the top of the desk and smiled down at her. "And he's never broken a promise?"

This time, her lip trembled the least little bit, but she controlled it almost before he saw. "No, sir. J. C. is a good boy. He isn't the kind to lay out all night and not go to work in the morning. He always comes right home 5:30 sharp unless I asked him to fetch some things at the store on his way. Something bad must have happened to him for him not to come home. Something real bad."

"And you're sure he didn't just go on to his job this morning?"

"I went by there first. Yesterday evening, they sent him to deliver a load of bricks. Said he never brought the company's truck back, and he never got there this morning. You've got to help me find him. J.C. is a good boy."

"All right. You take a seat over there, and I'll get one of the officers on duty to come talk to you."

"Yes, sir."

She perched in a chair next to one of the regular girls who had been brought in for streetwalking again and was just waiting to be booked. Holding herself straight as a queen, the old woman looked like a swan sitting next to a buzzard. Her grandson was probably laid out somewhere in a ditch, but the desk sergeant hoped not. He really hoped not.

He stuck his head into the duty room. "Hey, Murphy."

"Yeah." The officer answered without looking up from his paperwork.

"Got an old colored woman out here says her grandson has gone missing."

"How many does that make this week?"

"This one's different."

At that, Murphy looked up. He gnawed the eraser end of his pencil, sighed, and put the papers aside. "All right. Bring her in."

———

WHILE J. C.'S GRANDMOTHER WAS STILL IN FRONT OF MURPHY'S DESK, the call came in to the station about a young colored man's body that had been found behind the Odeon Theatre. It could have been anyone, but Murphy had one of what his mother called her bad Irish feelings about it.

"Mrs. Alphonse, I've go to go out on this call, but I'll be in touch as soon as we know anything about your grandson. Do you need a ride home?"

"No, sir. Thank you. I drove down in my Model T."

Something in the tilt of her head made him choke back the

wisecrack about her legs not being long enough to reach the gas that might have spilled out had someone else been in her place.

"All right then. We'll be in touch."

"You're going to find my J.C., aren't you?"

"We'll do everything we can."

"Now, remember, when you do, he's deaf. Been that way since the day he was born. You don't get right in front of him, he won't be able to understand what you're saying. Make sure your men know that."

"I'll make a note right here in the report."

"Thank you, Officer Murphy."

He watched her walk out, tapping the end of his pencil against the desktop as he thought. The Odeon. That was where Acker's victim showed up. Had to mean something that the new corpse was there, too.

Murphy scraped his chair back and went to the door of Acker's office, where the sergeant was just putting his hat on.

"Heading down to the Odeon to check out the new stiff?" Murphy said.

"Want to come along?" Acker said, tucking a notebook into his jacket pocket.

"Yep. I think I know who it is."

"You getting psychic powers?"

"Old colored woman was just in here. Her deaf grandson."

The sergeant gave him a sharp look. "Grab your hat, then, and come on."

CHAPTER 19

Unlike Calpurnia Waters, who had been curled around herself like a sleeping child, J. C. Alphonse lay stretched out on his back, staring wide-eyed but unseeing up at the sky. His lips were slightly parted in what might been the beginnings of a smile. Or the end of a scream.

Doc Mills stood and nodded to Acker. "Want to take a look?"

The sergeant crouched over the body. The boy couldn't have been much older than 18, if he was that. He lifted the jacket, felt inside, and extracted a battered wallet, the cheap kind you could get at the dime store. Flipped it open. A dollar bill, a ticket stub from the Amazing Waldo's show, a bus pass, and a picture of an older woman.

He handed the photo to Murphy, who studied it, shook his head, and passed it back to the sergeant.

"That's the grandmother," the officer said. He pointed to the body on the ground. "So, that has to be J. C." He crouched next to Acker for a closer look. "Dammit to hell. I'm not looking forward to telling her we found him."

Acker and Murphy stood.

"I'll go along if you want. Might help make the connection between this boy and the Waters woman. This one was at one of The Amazing Waldo's shows, too." He turned to the ambulance crew. "All right, boys. You can take him now. You'll phone me when your report is ready, won't you, Doc?"

"That very minute."

"Appreciate it."

As the sergeant had done when they found Calpurnia, Acker and Murphy walked the alley. Again, nothing out of the ordinary.

"He's not killing them here," Acker said. "Somebody would have seen or heard something, even down here. Just why he's leaving their bodies at the theatre is beyond me, though. If it is this magician, he'd have to be crazy as a loon to haul them out back where he's doing his show. Why not just dump them in the river and let the Mississippi carry them off?"

"Beats me. He must want us to find them."

"Well, when we catch him, we'll just have to ask him, won't we?"

IN THE SEWING ROOM AT THE MARCHAND HOUSE, BESS WAS DARNING socks for Jenkins, and Nell was reading the latest Agatha Christie. She had developed a taste for Christie after she and Calendar had solved the mystery of the missing Ginny Evans. Bess preferred Chesterton's Father Brown stories, but she liked helping her daughter-in-law unravel Christie's clues.

"Lord have mercy," Hattie said, charging into the room. "The police have found J. C. Alphonse dead. I don't know what his grandmama is going to do now. J. C. was the only one she had left in the world. Raised him since he was a baby. His mama and daddy got killed in a car wreck driving up to Chicago so his daddy could look for a job after he got to be such a drunk that nobody in Memphis would hire him anymore. Only thing that kept Mrs. Alphonse from taking to her grave was having those boys to look after."

Nell put aside her book and motioned for Hattie to sit beside her. "J. C. Alphonse. Is he that deaf boy who came and helped Jenkins with the yard work last summer? And his grandmother goes to Beale Street Baptist with you. We saw her at the funeral. Oh, Hattie."

"Nell, what on earth is going on up in here? First Calpurnia dead, and now that poor, sweet J. C." Hattie wiped furiously at her eyes. "I'm going to finish frying up this chicken I got on the stove so I can take it over to Mrs. Alphonse and sit with her for a while. This is just about going to kill her. We can have some of that leftover pimento cheese for our supper."

"I'm so sorry, Hattie. I'll ask Jenkins to take you."

First a crippled woman and now a deaf boy. Whatever the connection between the two, Nell was positive the murders weren't random.

CHAPTER 20

Simon appeared at the doorway of Joseph Calendar's study. "Miss Nell Marchand is on the phone for you, Dr. Calendar."

"Thank you, Simon." He lifted the receiver on the set on his desk and waited for Simon to hang up the hall phone. It was perhaps an extravagance to have two telephones in the house, but the sensitive nature of his work demanded a place he could speak with his clients in private. He knew Nell Marchand was not fond of the telephone—she said she wanted to be able to see the people she was talking to because she learned more from observing their faces than from what they said— so if she herself called again, something serious must have happened.

"Miss Nell, have you had news?"

"There's been another murder. A young man from Hattie's church. That's two now from Beale Street Baptist. I haven't said anything to her yet, but I have to wonder if someone is targeting people from her congregation."

"Two doesn't make a trend, but I don't believe in coincidence. We wouldn't want to wait for a third death from there to confirm the trend. Have you spoken to Sergeant Acker?"

"Not yet. Jenkins has taken Hattie to call on the boy's grandmother, but when they come back, I want to go down to the station to talk to the sergeant in person."

"May I accompany you? If you like, Simon and I can come for you and drive you downtown."

"Oh, yes, please. I can be ready in 15 minutes."

"We'll be right there." Calendar returned the receiver to its cradle and went to the door of his study to summon his butler. "Simon."

"Yes, Doctor?" The butler appeared in the hall wearing his apron. The cook had asked for the morning off, and Simon had no doubt been preparing a light luncheon for them.

"We'll need the car. We're going to pick up Mrs. Marchand and drive her down to police headquarters."

"Yes, sir. Right away."

"I'll meet you out front. Don't bother with changing into your chauffeur's coat."

"Yes, sir, Dr. Calendar." Simon was already stripping off the apron and disappearing into the kitchen, probably to turn off whatever was cooking on the stove or to store their luncheon in the ice box. The man was a treasure, and Calendar thanked his lucky stars for the day he had found him. Naturally gifted in managing a household, he had acquired even more polish and efficiency over the years, studying and improving himself until he was a butler-driver-secretary that all who knew of him envied.

A few moments later, the medium's burgundy 1933 Chrysler CL Imperial Dual Cowl Phaeton crunched across the gravel drive and pulled to a stop at the base of the front steps. The car had definitely been an indulgence, perhaps, but it was beautiful, and Calendar told himself that riding a fine car with his Negro manservant at the wheel told Memphis society that he was prosperous. He doubted that many would put much faith in a medium who drove himself around in a rundown rattletrap. Calendar slid onto the back seat, and Simon pulled away.

The ride to Nell Marchand's house was brief. When they arrived at the Marchand mansion on Poplar, Calendar could not help smiling at finding her waiting for them on the front steps. When Nell made up her mind about something, she acted. It was one of the many qualities that endeared her to him.

Calendar got out of the car himself to help Nell in. He then walked around to the other side, where Simon had opened his door for him and got back in. Simon understood that Calendar would wish to show Nell that courtesy himself, but he wasn't about to allow his employer to open his own car door.

"Good morning, Simon," Nell said when the driver had taken his place behind the wheel again. "How are you this morning?"

"Just fine, Miss Nell. You doing all right?"

Calendar smiled again. With most people, Simon was meticulously proper and spoke formally, but with Nell, the butler let his Georgia roots show.

"We're having much too much unhappiness at my house these days, I'm afraid," she said. "Has Dr. Calendar told you about the death of my Hattie's friend and now of this young man from her church?"

"Yes, ma'am, and I hope you will let Hattie know just how sorry I am. It is a sad, sad day."

"Thank you, Simon. I will."

"To police headquarters, then, Simon," Calendar said. "We're going to get to work on finding who is doing this and stopping him."

"Yes, sir." Simon didn't exactly peel away from Nell's front steps, but he did punch the accelerator hard enough for the Imperial to shoot into the traffic on Poplar Avenue, headed toward the police station downtown.

At the sound of a soft knock, Sergeant Arnold Acker looked up from his desk to find Nell Marchand and Joseph Calendar standing in the doorway.

"I hope you don't mind our coming in unannounced, Sergeant," Nell said. "I told the officer at the front desk that you were expecting us, and he said to come on back. I thought that would save him the time and trouble of letting you know."

"Of course not, Miss Nell. We're old friends now. No need to worry about procedures. Come in, please. Dr. Calendar."

Acker pulled out a chair for Nell and waited until she had seated herself before he returned to his own chair behind the desk. Calendar took the second chair beside her.

"We've heard about J. C. Alphonse," she said without preamble.

"Bad news travels fast," Acker said. "Officer Murphy and I were just over at his grandmother's house, telling her we'd found him."

"Did you know that Mrs. Alphonse also goes to Beale Street Baptist with Hattie?" She paused to glance at Calendar. "We thought there might be a connection somehow to what happened to Calpurnia Waters. She also worshipped at Beale Street."

"Have mercy," Acker said. "Hattie must be torn up about this boy, too."

"She's distressed, of course. She has known him and his people all his life. You know how churches are about their members. As far as they're concerned, it's all one big family."

"Unh, unh, unh. Well, I am sure sorry about that." Acker made a note on the pad on his desk. "We hadn't gotten far enough with the boy's grandmother to find that out yet. Couldn't tell us much this morning, as you can imagine. We asked her to come in after she'd had a chance to arrange for J.C.'s funeral and alert the rest of her folks. Murphy offered to pick her up so she wouldn't have to negotiate downtown traffic. He has taken a shine to Mrs. Alphonse."

"J. C. is . . . was the only family she has in Memphis, Hattie says. I don't know about anywhere else."

"Bless her heart." Acker flipped through his notes, wrote "family?" next to Mrs. Alphonse's name.

Nell waited for him to look up again. "Dr. Calendar and I agree that there may be some link between the two killings even beyond Beale Street Baptist."

The sergeant had grown to like and admire Nell Marchand, to think of her as almost a friend. She was smart and tenacious and big-hearted, and the Evans girl might still be missing had Mrs. Marchand not insisted that she was alive and persisted in looking for her, even after Boss Crump and everyone else had warned her off. That did not, however, mean that Acker wanted her involving herself in police work again and getting herself in the middle of this case any more than she already was over Calpurnia Waters.

"That's certainly possible, Miss Nell. It's something we'll look at. We'll also look for other similarities between the victims. Don't you worry. I'm making this my Number One case."

"If the church is the key, that would account for some of what they have in common. Beyond being handicapped, that is."

"Yes, ma'am. Those are the obvious similarities. The church doesn't account for that connection, though. You leave everything to me. I'll get to the bottom of it, if it's the last thing I do." He wasn't about to tell her that J.C. Alphonse had also been to one of the Amazing Waldo's performances.

"I'm sure Dr. Calendar and I could be of help in your investigation."

"Maybe so, Miss Nell, but I would feel a whole lot better if you'd let the Memphis police deal with this. Remember, this is a murder case, and now we have two victims."

"I'm a big girl, Sergeant. I think I can take care of myself."

"Yes, ma'am. I've seen you at work, and I have no doubt of that. I'm always glad to listen to your theories. And I understand that you have a personal stake in this, Hattie knowing both of the deceased and all. But you need to leave going after whoever is doing this killing to us."

"What you mean to say is that you don't want me interfering."

"Now, that's not exactly what I said. But if you're out there messing around, our murderer might get scared enough that we'll never catch him. Or he might come after you. If he thinks someone's about to find him out, he just might decide he needs to do away with that person, too. I don't want to think of you putting yourself in any danger. I'm sure Dr. Calendar here is with me on wanting to keep you safe."

Nell and the sergeant both looked at Calendar, who smiled an enigmatic smile. "Miss Nell's safety has always been my concern."

At that, Nell was silent, but Acker had seen that look in her eye before, and that look meant nothing but trouble.

CHAPTER 21

Back from the police station, Nell went in search of her mother-in-law, whom she discovered in the back parlor, reading the Press-Scimitar, with the other Memphis daily, the Commercial Appeal, stacked at her feet. Bess's late husband the Judge had read both papers because it was good policy to keep up with what everybody was thinking, he always said. His widow continued his habit.

"Did you see in the paper that they caught that Barnes boy?" Bess said, clicking her tongue. "He goes by Machine Gun Kelly now, which must be a relief to his poor mother. I mean the name, not that they caught him. Of course, everybody in Memphis knows who he is, and she's bound to be mortified all the same. And they're nice people, the Barneses. They went to our church for the longest time. I never will understand what happened to him."

"I'm sorry, Mother," Nell said. "What did you say?"

"Machine Gun Kelly. They caught him and that tacky wife of his right here in Memphis. They were hiding in a house over on Rayner Street." Bess turned the paper toward Nell for her to look at the mug shots of Kelly and his wife, who looked smug and, yes, a little tacky in a suit jacket with black feathers at the shoulders.

"Oh." Nell sank down on the sofa next to Bess and pretended to read the headline her mother-in-law held under her nose. "Well, at least they've caught someone."

Bess lowered the paper to her lap. She reached for Nell's hand and took it gently in hers. "I know what's on your mind, child. Between you and Hattie, I feel like the only person awake in this house. Why don't you tell me about it?"

Nell hesitated, sighed, and leaned against her mother-in-law for comfort. "I'm worried to death about Hattie, Mother. I'm about to fly all to pieces, but I can't because she already is. She can't even rouse herself to go down to my salon. I have to be Madame Nelora all by myself, which I can, of course, but you know how much she enjoys greeting my clients and showing them into my reading room. She's grieving Calpurnia so, and there doesn't seem to be a thing I can do about it. The police don't have the first idea about how to find who killed her. And now this poor Alphonse boy has been murdered, too."

"Yes, it's horrible. That poor child." Bess gave Nell's hand a quick squeeze. "I wonder what's happened to people. All these gangsters and their machine guns in the papers all the time and people we know turning up dead. But Hattie will heal, sweet girl. That's the way of grief. It ebbs away until one day it's a gentle lapping on the shore instead of that terrible wave that crashes over you until you know you'll drown."

She opened the locket she always wore around her neck and looked at the picture of the Judge inside it. "When my Daniel passed, I thought I wanted to jump right down into his grave with him. Just putting one foot in front of the other took every ounce of strength I had. But every day, I was a little better, a little stronger. And now that I have Dr. Calendar and can speak to Daniel whenever I want, why, I know he's still with me. Calpurnia will always be with Hattie."

Nell kissed Bess on the cheek. "I hope so."

"And don't you worry about finding whoever is doing this. The Lord won't let such evil go on. There will be a way to stop it."

"I know, Mother, but I don't think Hattie can rest until there is. Even she has a breaking point, and I'm afraid she's almost there. And she's too bull-headed to admit it."

"She wouldn't be Hattie if she were any other way."

"No, she wouldn't." Nell smiled. "Now, I'd better go see if she's got everything she needs for supper. Much as I love pimento cheese, I don't much want it again for supper. Jenkins asked for the night off, but he can run to the store right quick, or I can scramble eggs and make toast."

"All right, love." Bess closed the locket and turned back to the story about Machine Gun Kelly and the exploits of the men of the Federal Bureau of Investigation, shaking her head and clucking her tongue again.

Pausing in the doorway, Nell glanced back at Bess. She had set the paper beside her and picked up her knitting as she read. If a big star like Fanny Bryce could make sweaters for the unemployed, all the members of the Nineteenth Century Club had decided they would, too. Bess's was cerulean because she said the unfortunates especially needed bright, cheerful colors. Of all the pain Ellis Marchand had visited on Nell in their marriage, at least by dying, he had bequeathed her his mother. Every day, she understood a little better how precious a gift that was.

CHAPTER 22

There had been a time when Sister Louise Henslowe had been the most famous preacher in the country. Her appearances had brought thousands of fervent believers to hear her. She had counted the great and near great among her friends. Devout followers had named their children after her.

The zeal that she inspired in people's hearts had loosened their purse strings, and the donations had flowed in abundance. That money, Sister Louise had used to open tabernacles in New York, Chicago, and Los Angeles. She lived well but not lavishly, those funds going, as she said, to sustain the humblest of God's children.

But as times changed and she grew older, fresher faces and newer styles of preaching began to challenge her. The crowds dwindled. Invitations to preach grew fewer. Gradually, she had to release more and more of her staff. One day, Henry came to tell her that she was almost broke. At last, she came home to Memphis to her original Tabernacle of Light. Here, she made her last stand.

Clad in her accustomed white robes and black stole, Sister Louise Henslowe wound down her sermon. It was time for the part of the Friday service at the Tabernacle that everyone had always come to see—the healing.

"And now, brothers and sisters, if there are any among you who need healing, any ready to offer up their hearts to the Lord and ask for His divine aid, step forward now."

A man rose from one of the aisle seats and began to make his way toward the front, leaning heavily on a cane and walking with such a pronounced, foot-dragging limp that it seemed to take him forever to make his way to the stage at Sister Louise's feet. She walked to the center of the stage and waited for him.

"Come forward, Brother. The Lord waits for you. Put your faith in His healing power and you will be made whole. As I am His instrument, you can trust and believe that you will be made whole."

The man reached the stage at her feet, and Sister Louise held out her microphone toward him.

"Tell us your name, Brother, and the nature of your affliction."

Leaning forward to reach the microphone, the man laid his hat on the stage. "I am Ted McCrory, and I lost my leg in the Second Battle of the Marne." He turned to face the audience, lifting up his right pant leg to show them the prosthetic limb beneath it. "I am ready to be healed, Sister Louise. Can you restore my leg?"

"Lordy, ain't no way even Sister could do that," someone in the congregation said. Murmurs of agreement rippled through the sanctuary.

She paused, breathless and thinking furiously. Of all the true miracles that she had performed in God's name, no one had ever asked her to replace a missing limb before. But if the Lord worked through her as He had so many times before, what an inspiration it would be to be able to add this man's artificial leg to her museum of no-longer-needed canes, crutches, and wheelchairs.

She looked out over the crowd, her eyes seeking and finding Henry. He shook his head slightly as though to warn her, but she beamed at him. With the Lord on her side, there was nothing she couldn't do. This was all she needed—one more miracle, her greatest, to restore her reputation and persuade sinners to let her guide them to the true path. Henry always worried too much.

She reached down to the lame man and clasped his raised hand in both of hers. Her rich, deep voice boomed out over the Tabernacle, filling every corner. "Brother McCrory, no miracle is too great for Our Lord Jesus Christ. His power knows no bounds. He is capable of all things seen and unseen. Make your way onto the stage so that I may lay my hands directly on your missing limb. Together, we will pray. Everyone here tonight will unite in prayer, and we will rejoice together when the Lord gives you a new leg."

She stood and motioned to her stagehands to help McCrory onstage. When he had joined her in the spotlight at the center, she turned to the audience. "Brothers and sisters, pray with me that this man may be restored and made whole." She knelt and wrapped her hands around his right leg, the plastic cool and smooth between them. "Brother Ted, are you ready?"

"I am," he said, his voice shaking.

"Then, Jesus, we ask You to send down Your healing love. Remember what this man has sacrificed for his country and for Your glory. As we put our faith in You, make him whole again."

The lights in the Tabernacle flickered. Evelina was the best stage manager in the world. She always understood just the right moment.

"Yes, Jesus," Sister Louise said, standing. She raised her arms heavenward. "I hear You, Lord." She stood and embraced the veteran. "Now, Brother, let us see if your faith has been great enough. Lift up your trouser leg." She turned to the audience, stretching her arms out wide to them as though saying, "Prepare to offer up all praise to the Lord."

Doing as he was told, McCrory revealed not the flesh-and-blood limb he had prayed for but the same artificial one that had born him so haltingly to the stage. A murmur of disappointment swept through the congregation.

"It ain't no different," came a voice from the crowd.

"He's still crippled," someone else said.

Sister Louise turned slowly and stared down at the leg, speechless for a moment. This man had come to her in need, and she had failed him. Then, she clenched her eyes tight and stretched her arms heavenward again. "Lord, it is we weak and black-hearted sinners who have failed Brother McCrory with our lack of belief, not You. Imperfect vessels that we are, I pray that You may heal each of us as You see fit and give us strength to carry out Your great work. Show Brother McCrory the way to accept Your plan for him. Grant him contentment with the lot he has been given. Bless him with the understanding that we cannot always know or understand what You intend for us. If You cannot grant him a body that is whole, we ask you to give him a spirit that is."

She took one of the man's hands and spoke so quietly to him that the congregation could not hear. "I'm sorry, Brother. Our faith has been found lacking, but do not let this turn you from the Lord."

Wiping his eyes, Ted McCrory nodded to her. He made his way back to the edge of the stage and haltingly down the steps, waving away the same stagehands who had helped him up them.

Sister Louise waited until he had returned to his seat before she held her arms out to the congregation again. "Who else? Be not cast down, brethren. Who else would step forward to be healed?"

Not a soul in the congregation stirred.

CHAPTER 23

Calendar woke in the night and sat bolt upright, the feeling of doom pressing so powerfully on him that he thought his heart must stop. "Nell!"

It took him several desperate gulps of air for him to remember that he was safe in his own bed. He leaned against the headboard, knowing sleep would not come again that night. It was an old, too familiar pattern. The dreams never left him.

Even with tears streaking her face, she was as beautiful as the light of the moon on the waters of the Nile.

Priestess of Isis and seer of renown, Tadinanefer looked up from the bedside of her only brother into the eyes of Sekhemib and beyond them to his heart.

"Please, Learned One, you must save him."

The young prince would live, but the physician sent to heal him was forever lost.

A devotee of the goddess, the queen brought Tadinanefer to the court to attend her. Sekhemib was senior apprentice to the royal chancellor and physician Imhotep, but she could never be his. She was too precious a prize for the sons of kings who wished to ally themselves with the mighty pharaoh Djoser. But Sekhemib found favor with her. In secret, they slipped away to the queen's gardens to meet.

"One day soon, the pharaoh will marry me to a princeling I have never seen. Then you will be lost to me forever."

Sekhemib stroked her hair. She leaned her cheek against his chest, and he enfolded her in his arms. "I will go to the queen," he said. "I will ask

90

her to release you. When her eldest boy was ill and no one, not even wise Imhotep, thought he would live, I healed him. That day, she promised me whatever boon I desired. I will remind her of her pledge. I think it is not too great a thing to ask, your love for her son's life."

"And if she cannot persuade the pharaoh?"

"Then we will flee to Sheba and make our lives there. There is always need of physicians in royal houses."

"I will go with you anywhere."

He kissed her.

Behind them, the darkness stirred. Nebi slipped from the shadows, his face a mask of envy and hate. He watched them a moment longer before he made his way back to the palace toward the king's chambers.

When the palace guard came for them, Sekhemib and Tadinanefer had time for a last kiss before they were torn apart and dragged into the great Djoser's presence.

The king leaned against the arm of his throne, his face a mask of displeasure. To his right sat the queen, her eyes cast downward. Looking grave, Imhotep stood at Djoser's right hand between the royal couple. The guard forced the lovers to their knees at pharaoh's feet. Both prostrated themselves, faces to the floor.

"Get up," the ruler said. When they had done so, he turned his gaze on Sekhemib. "What penalty does the law require that I visit on you for daring to touch a princess of the blood?"

"Death, my lord," Sekhemib said. "But I beg you to punish me and let Tadinanefer go. As Isis loved Osiris, I pray the goddess may plant such mercy in your heart."

"Husband," the queen said, kneeling at his side. "Remember that your son would lie with our ancestors were it not for Sekhemib's healing powers. Instead, he grows straight and strong to carry on your house.

"And the girl is child of our sister. Her blood is ours. Her only offense is to love this man as I love you. Show that you are a merciful king, that you rule your people with a kind heart as well as a strong hand.

"When he made our son well, I pledged Sekhemib a boon, but he asked

nothing more than to serve us. He has done so loyally and well always. Grant me leave to give him his life and Tadinanefer's."

The king stretched out his hand to his wife. She pressed her forehead to the back of it. He rose, pulling her to her feet with him. He held out his other hand to Tadinanefer, who drew near and pressed her forehead to it as well.

"Child, why should I spare you?"

"Because you are merciful and great, as your lady has said."

"You have defied my wishes."

"Yes, my lord uncle, and for that, I beg your pardon."

"And if I choose to spare only one life?"

"Then take mine, and let Sekhemib live." Now she kissed the back of the king's hand and knelt in front of him.

Sekhemib stepped forward, "My lord, no. Take my life for hers."

The king turned to Imhotep. "Can you spare this man?"

The healer bowed. "My lord, he is not without skill. I had thought to have him follow me as your physician, but if you demand his life, then it must be forfeit."

Pharaoh smiled. Still holding Tadinanefer's hand, he took Sekhemib's in his other. "As you returned my son's life to me, so I give yours to you. As my queen has pled for this girl, so I grant her hers. My word is the law of this land, and as measure of my greatness, I show mercy to you both." He passed Tadinanefer's hand to Sekhemib. "Take her, and bear many sons for Egypt."

"My king is merciful, indeed," Sekhemib said.

"I am weary and would return to my bed." The pharaoh turned to his queen. "Come, wife, and remind me what it is to be young and in love."

"Thank you, my lord," Tadinanefer said. "My lady."

"Tomorrow, we will speak to the high priestess of Isis, and all will be well," the queen said. "There are girls enough of royal blood, and we will choose another for the Hittite prince. For now, Sekhemib, escort her to my chambers."

Tadinanefer and Sekhemib bowed to the royal couple. Outside the audience chamber, Nebi stepped from the shadows behind them, a dagger in his hand. He struck Sekhemib between the shoulders, driving the blade in to the hilt. Sekhemib fell, Tadinanefer screamed, and Nebi fled from the hall. The palace guard came at a run.

Tadinanefer cradled Sekhemib in her arms. He smiled at her, the light already beginning to fade from his eyes. "I will love you forever."

"You are my life!" She kissed him. "I will come with you."

"No, my heart, you must live. We will see each other again in the afterlife. I will wait for you."

"No!"

"Promise me so I may go in peace."

She kissed him again, nodded. "I will come."

"I will wait."

The queen pulled Tadinanefer gently away so that Imhotep could gather up Sekhemib's body and bear it away to be prepared.

The girl watched them out of sight before she sank again to her knees. "Isis!" she cried. "Queen of Heaven, great Mother of the Gods, bring him back to me. As you rescued your husband Osiris from the underworld, restore my love to me, I beg you. I will serve you all my days, only bring him back to me."

The goddess took form before her, filling the hall with light. And as clearly as she heard the queen's voice murmuring in her ear, Tadinanefer heard Isis speak. "Not in this life, child, but in those to come. That is the gift I give you, and the curse, that you will seek each other lifetime after lifetime. When he finds you, he may never speak your true name, and you will never know him until he does."

And thus it began. The same scenes playing over and over again, lifetime after lifetime, ending always in death.

CHAPTER 24

So early that it was almost indecent, Joseph Calendar presented himself at Nell's door. She answered his knock herself and asked him to join the family for breakfast.

The two took their coffee to her sitting room, discussing again what her vision might mean and how best to approach a reading. Calendar stood by the fire Nell had asked Jenkins to build against the first chill of autumn. She loved the fall for the bright leaves that festooned the trees and the cool nights that let her burrow deep under the covers and sleep the soundest sleeps she knew. But fires in the fireplace were her favorite thing of all. They made her think of her father, who always wanted a fire going morning to night the minute it was even remotely chilly enough to allow one.

"Nell, I'm not sure you should attempt a reading around these killings. In fact, I don't think you should investigate them any further."

Her mouth fell open, and her coffee cup stopped halfway on its journey to her lips. "I can't believe it. After all these months of your telling me I can learn to control my gift, that it's a responsibility I cannot shirk. But now when it's Hattie I want to help, when she's grieving over poor Calpurnia in a way she never has over anyone or anything else, you want me to turn my back on her? You know I can't do that. Not to her. I have to try every way possible to find out who killed Calpurnia and the Alphonse boy. That's the only way Hattie will rest."

Now, Calendar came to sit beside her and took her hand, a gesture so rare in the last months that Nell almost started. He looked into her face as though seeking the answers to unasked questions there. "This case may be dangerous for you. You have felt it yourself. If anything happened to you . . . ." He gripped her hand to the point of pain. She extracted it gently from his grasp.

"Isn't overlooking danger part of managing my visions?"

Apparently aware that he had been leaning over her, he sat back and withdrew his hand. He looked like a drowning man coming up for the last time, almost wild and unable to control whatever emotion had overtaken him. Nell had never seen him this way before.

"Joseph? Are you all right?"

She watched him work his will on himself, slowing his breathing and returning to the calm center that was the version of him that she knew and trusted best. Then, it was done, and he seemed himself again, poised, controlled, his eyes almost hooded.

"My apologies. In my concern for you, I forgot myself for a moment."

"It's all right, but I was worried for you."

"Forgive me for frightening you."

"I wasn't frightened for myself. You seemed . . . unlike yourself. Like someone I don't know."

Calendar regarded her quietly, thinking. "Nell, if I tell you that you might be in real, perhaps mortal, danger, will you trust me? Will you let me guide you?"

"As long as you don't ask me to stop helping Hattie. This isn't the first time we've faced difficulties."

"What we're facing are more than difficulties."

"Joseph."

He paused again. "Very well. I know I cannot prevent you from pursuing this murderer, but will you promise to send for me the moment something untoward happens?"

"How will I be able to tell that from an ordinary, every-day, run-of-the-mill vision?"

At that, Calendar managed a smile in return. "I see your point."

"And you know I'm bound to consult you about anything to do with this whole business."

"And you know that I am always yours to command. But Nell, please, if you feel even the slightest menace directed at you yourself, you must come to me at once."

"I promise." Nell studied him. "Is there some particular reason you think such a thing will happen?"

"There are ancient forces that may be at work here. Forces that may want to destroy your power. Or you. It is beyond my ability to tell you more. All I can do is try to protect you."

She shivered. Calendar's fear was somehow much worse than her own. Part of her wanted to turn away, to agree that she would go no further in trying to discover who had murdered Calpurnia, to run and hide. But she could not abandon Hattie. Hattie who had never thought of leaving her, no matter how desperate her circumstances. Whatever came, it was hers to face.

CHAPTER 25

A devout Christian and member in good standing of Beale Street Baptist Church, Aunt Mary Rudolph, the hoodoo doctor, headed the church widows and orphans committee, helped with the annual bazaar, and sang in the choir. She was also a close friend and ally of Brother Cage, Beale Street's pastor, who had been known to consult her himself. When word reached her that poor J.C. Alphonse had been murdered, she went to the minister and offered to cast a protecting spell over Beale Street Baptist and its congregation. Believing that if a little supernatural help was a good thing, a lot was even better, Brother Cage agreed.

From the pulpit, he was ready to move on to his Sunday sermon on the importance of community and mutual support as soon as he finished delivering the church announcements.

"Brethren, you all know Sister Mary Rudolph, who has long been a pillar of our church community." He paused for the chorus of amens, turning to nod at Aunt Mary where she sat in the choir. "You also know that Sister Mary is a practicing hoodoo doctor, which has never in any way interfered with her worship here. And you know that this community has lost two members at the hands of a murderer.

"Now, no one is saying that Calpurnia Waters and J.C. Alphonse were struck down because they were members of this church, but Sister Mary has offered to use her hoodoo abilities to encircle Beale Street with the kind of protecting love that we all know Jesus would want us to have. She will call on the Blood of Jesus to ward off evil. Any of you who would like to take part in that protecting spell are welcome to stay on after today's service. Those of you who do not wish to participate may, of course, leave after the benediction."

After the service, hoodoo doctor and pastor were both pleased to see that all the members of Beale Street Baptist wanted her protection.

Aunt Mary slipped off her choir robe and extracted from the tote sack she had brought with her a mason jar filled with egg shells she had ground into a fine powder and an enormous bundle of rue. She passed around the edge of the sanctuary, sprinkling the powder at all the doors and windows. With the rue, she made the sign of the cross on the forehead of each member of the congregation. To each she gave a sprig of the plant, cautioning each to carry it until the danger had passed.

When everyone in the congregation had been so blessed, Brother Cage said, "Hallelujah!" and had them all recite The Lord's Prayer together before he sent them home.

———

On her way back to the Marchand house from church, Hattie detoured to the Zion Cemetery for a visit with Calpurnia. She was buried next to her daddy, so Hattie settled on his tombstone to talk to her.

"I guess you know somebody took poor J. C. Alphonse, too. They found him out behind the Odeon Theatre, right where they found you. Bound to have been the same somebody. Nell, Dr. Calendar, and I have been figuring on who it is, but if you know who killed y'all, could you please whisper something to Nell so it shows up good and clear in one of her visions? I hate to think he might get hold of somebody else.

"But don't you worry about Beale Street. Aunt Mary Rudolph just put a protecting spell on all of us, so we're going to be just fine."

Hattie took off her church hat and set it next to her on the tombstone.

"Now that you're up there in heaven, I know at least you got your legs back. Remember how we used to run in home from school in the afternoons? Mama would always have a piece of cornbread or pie or some cookies and a big glass of milk waiting for us. Then, she'd make us do our homework until it was time for your mama or daddy to come get you."

She could see Cal charging ahead of her to push through the back door at the old Leyton house and plop herself down at the kitchen table.

"Well, hello there, Miss Calpurnia," Hattie's mama would say, just like she was addressing the queen of England. "And how are you today?"

"Just fine, Mrs. Taylor," Cal would reply. "And you?"

"Why, I am just as fine as a frog hair split three ways, thank you very much."

And Cal would laugh every time, just like she was hearing Mama's awful old joke for the first time.

In the summer, Calpurnia came to spend the week days with Hattie. Her mama worked cleaning houses, and her daddy had a job at the Co'cola bottling plant, so Hattie's mother kept her. On Mondays, Wilhelmina Taylor had the day off, so Mondays were what they called their adventure days. Sometimes Mama took them to the swimming pool. Although she would never admit it, Hattie was a little afraid of the water. The best she ever managed was a dog paddle.

But Cal, Cal could swim like a fish. She was fearless enough to jump off the high diving board, the only girl with the nerve to try it. And she didn't do a cannonball like the boys. She would dive, as elegant as a swan swooping down through the air to cut the water with only the smallest splash.

When they were old enough, Cal and Hattie got jobs working in the refreshment stand at the pool. Hattie's mother made sandwiches for them to sell. There was ice cream they dipped from a small freezer at the back and a hot plate where they boiled hotdogs that split open in the water while they cooked and were so good that Hattie sometimes ate two. Cal could eat anything. She was a bottomless pit, Hattie's mother always said. "Never did see a girl who could eat like that Cal."

Even after she was sick, they still had their adventure Mondays. Hattie's mother took them to the movies, where they sat in the balcony and laughed at Charlie Chaplin and Buster Keaton. Cal always had a nickel to spend on candy or pickles. She didn't like popcorn, which Hattie could eat by the bushel, because she said the hulls stuck in her teeth and made her cough.

In the summers, the pool manager set up a special table so Cal could still run the cash register. When their shifts ended, Hattie helped her change into her bathing suit before she settled her on a lounge chair under one of the umbrellas. When it got too hot, one of the lifeguards would lower her into the water and let her float, keeping one hand behind her head and the other at the small of her back so she could stretch out in the water and look up at the clouds.

"I sure do miss you, Cal," Hattie said. "You know Leb already sold the house and moved Miss Ruby up to Illinois. Makes me sad every time I pass it, knowing I can't just knock on the door and find you home.

"But don't you worry. We're going to find out who killed you and left you in that alley like some piece of trash to be thrown out. Whatever the police do, you know I'm not ever going to give up on you. Got my Nell working on it, too, and Dr. Calendar. You met him last time you were at the house, remember? He kept finding excuses to come into the kitchen so he could break off a corner of cornbread or get a piece of chicken.

"Dr. Calendar is a fine gentleman. I know Nell thinks she doesn't need to get married again, but I can't help hoping that one day she opens her eyes and sees just how fine he is."

The sun disappeared behind a cloud, and Hattie shivered. She stood, dusting off her seat. "Well, I guess I'd better get on home and start thinking about what to fix for supper. I'll see you again next Sunday."

At the graveyard gate, she stopped to look back over her shoulder.

Just beyond Calpurnia's grave, she could see the fresh-turned earth of
J. C.'s. Neither one of them had ever done a mean thing in their lives.
She was going to find out what happened to both of them, if it cost her
very last breath.

CHAPTER 26

The Sunday matinee behind him, the Amazing Waldo stepped into a nondescript diner with red-checked oil-cloth tablecloths not far from the Odeon to gather strength for his evening performance. The place might be humble, but the food was cheap and good. Room service had its uses, but from time to time Waldo relished a break for real food.

He asked for a booth in the back and sat facing away from the door. Once settled, he ordered smothered chicken with rice and gravy and a Coke. The waitress had just put a basket of fresh rolls and butter in front of him when Ted McCrory slipped into the booth across from him and reached for one.

"How'd it go?" Waldo said.

"You should have been there." McCrory grinned around a bite of roll. "Took the wind right out of her sails. After I dragged my poor, broke-down self back to my seat, not a single person came up to be healed. But I'll give her this. Sister Louise is one persuasive woman. Up there at the altar, she just about had me believing I could grow myself a new leg if I could pray hard enough."

"Excellent." Waldo slid an envelope across the table to him. "Be sure you're in the audience tonight. Who knows? I might find some magical solution for your problem."

"Thank you kindly." Opening the envelope, McCrory ran his thumb across the edge of the bills inside and nodded to himself before he slid the money into his jacket pocket. "What do you have against Sister Louise anyway? Seems like she does help some folks."

The waitress arrived with a fragrant plate of chicken and an enormous scoop of rice that she set in front of Waldo. She turned to McCrory. "You gonna order something, honey?"

"Just coffee, ma'am, please."

"Comin' right up." She shuffled away.

"Let's just say Louise Henslowe and I go way back. I owe her a favor."

"Old girlfriend, huh?"

"Not exactly. Anyway, she and that underling of hers have been hanging around my performances a little too much for my taste. I want to give her something else to think about, take a bit more wind out of her sails, as you say."

The waitress set a steaming cup in front of McCrory, who spooned in three spoons of sugar and added a glug of cream. He wrapped his hands around the coffee as though trying to warm them, lifted it to his mouth, sipped, and smacked his lips. "How about springing for some supper?"

"There's enough in that envelope to buy you all the suppers you can eat for the foreseeable future." Waldo extracted his wallet and fished out a five. He pushed it across the table to McCrory, who grabbed it and stuck it in his pocket. "But here. Go buy yourself a steak dinner. I don't want to risk anyone seeing me with you before tonight's show. Or after, for that matter."

McCrory shrugged, took another hearty slug of his coffee. "Come to think of it, a steak sounds mighty good." He pushed himself to his feet, dragging his right leg after him. "See you tonight."

Waldo listened to the sound of the man clumping away. When he was out of earshot, he tucked the napkin in his lap, poured gravy over the chicken and rice, and forked up a generous bite. The cooking was one of his favorite things about tours through the South. He would miss it when he left Memphis.

CHAPTER 27

As though word had spread that the Amazing Waldo would perform a particularly astonishing feat at that evening's performance, a standing-room-only audience crowded the theatre. This time, Joseph Calendar had taken a seat near the front where he could observe more closely.

The magician ran through his usual repertoire—reading minds, shredding a man's handkerchief and returning it to him whole, making Penelope float in the air. The crowd grew restive, not knowing exactly what it was they had come to see but eager to get to it. Waldo himself seemed to be sleepwalking through the performance, his usual verve and panache missing.

"None of this is real," a voice suddenly called from the back of the theatre. "It's all a bunch of cheap tricks anybody could do."

In the middle of transforming his cane into a snake, the conjurer paused and peered in the direction of the voice. "Is that so? Well, then, good sir, I challenge you to join me on the stage and assist me with my next illusion. Or, better yet, I defy you to perform it yourself."

"You got it, pal!"

The heckler stepped into the aisle and made his way haltingly toward the stage, his right leg obviously encumbered in some way. When he reached it, his progress up the steps was painful to watch. Taking his place beside the magician, he looked winded and leaned hard on his walking stick.

"Well, then, my fine friend," Waldo said, shaking his hand, "you doubt the existence of magic. I hope we will be able to make a believer of you."

"I wouldn't count on it."

"Would you tell us your name, please, sir?"

"McCrory. Name's Ted McCrory."

"And where do you come from, Mr. McCrory?"

"Well, I sure didn't fall off a turnip truck, if that's what you want to know."

Waldo didn't respond but took a top hat from the tray that bore his props. He showed it to McCrory, who stuck first his nose and then his hand into it. The conjurer then held it out to the crowd so that they could see it was empty. He placed the hat on the table his assistant had brought to the front of the stage, waved his wand under the table to show there was nothing there. Then he tapped the hat three times with his wand, reached inside, and pulled out a bouquet of roses, which he presented to Penelope.

"There's a hidden compartment under there," McCrory said. "That hat has a false bottom to it, and you just reached through there to get the flowers."

"Would you like to examine the hat more closely?" Waldo held it out.

The man grabbed the hat from him. "Look here." He jammed his fist into it, trying to punch through the bottom, but the hat didn't give.

At that, the magician simply raised an eyebrow and smiled out at the crowd, which responded with titters that grew into guffaws.

"That was easy. Anybody could have done that trick. I saw a fella do it at the carnival back home."

"Perhaps we should attempt something more challenging, then," Waldo said. "Forgive me, sir, but may I ask you what happened to your leg? I couldn't help noticing that you walk with some difficulty."

"German grenade took it off." The man pulled up his pant leg to reveal an artificial limb that replaced his leg from the knee down. "Left me with this one." He rapped the plastic with a knuckle.

"What if I told you I could send you back in time, back to before you lost your leg?"

McCrory snorted. "I'd say you're crazy."

"But, if I could do it, would you go? If I could restore your leg to you, would you be willing to take the chance?"

"In a New York minute."

The illusionist gestured to Penelope, who hurried to his side. "Prepare the case," he said.

She nodded to stagehands waiting in the wings on either side. The two men hurried to the back, where the ancient coffin into which Calpurnia Waters had disappeared waited. They wheeled it to Waldo's side. Penelope opened the cover and stepped aside.

"Mr. McCrory, this case once housed the remains of an Egyptian magician so powerful that it is said he escaped death's embrace to live again. It has been handed down through the centuries from one of his spiritual descendants to the next until, at last, it has come to me. It is said that this case contains powers beyond our imagining. Will you chance calling on those powers?"

Staring at Waldo, the man stood stock still, the battle between doubt and credulity written across his features. At last, he spoke. "You mean to tell me that if I get in that case, I'm going to come back with my own leg?"

"That is my hope. A spell this powerful can be difficult to conjure, but if everyone in the audience will concentrate along with you, we may be able to summon it. Are you willing to try?"

"If there's a chance in hell I'll get my leg back, you bet your life, I will."

The man made a move toward the case, but Waldo put up a hand to restrain him. "Be aware, Mr. McCrory, that this spell is not without risk. As the fine people of Memphis have already seen, there is a chance that something unimagined could happen."

"Mister, I don't care. You can't know what it's like to drag yourself around like this every day."

"Very well, then. Penelope, assist our friend here into the case."

Waldo's assistant helped the subject back himself into the mummy case and instructed him to cross his arms across his chest.

The magician put his hand on the cover of the case. "Last chance to change your mind."

"Get on with it."

He closed the case and turned to the audience. "Ladies and gentlemen, concentrate. We must all focus on sending this man back to his old self and returning him safely. I need the power of your minds joining with my own to accomplish this transformation. Concentrate!"

He rapped on the cover of the case three times. Then stepped back. "Penelope."

His assistant pulled back the cover to reveal that the case was empty. Waldo stepped to it, seeming surprised. He walked around it as though looking for McCrory. "Ladies and gentlemen, as you can clearly see, Mr. McCrory seems to have vanished. I'm going to close the cover again and hope that we can summon his spirit and body back from the realms to which we have sent him. Again, I ask you to concentrate."

He struck the cover again. He motioned to Penelope, who opened it, only to reveal that it was empty still. "Good people," Waldo said, his face a mask of regret. "I don't know what to tell you, but I believe Mr. McCrory may have vanished for good. We can only hope that in whatever realm he has reached, he has been made whole again."

"Here I am," came a cry from the rear of the theater. Everyone turned toward the voice. McCrory appeared in the aisle, standing straight as an arrow, his cane gone. "I'm right here." Then he sprinted toward the stage. Members of the audience gasped. When he reached the stage, he leapt lightly onto it with the ease and grace of a dancer.

"Look!" he said. He pulled up his pant leg to reveal a normal, muscular, flesh-and-blood leg where moments before there had been an artificial limb. "My leg. I got my leg back, good as new."

The audience began to applaud, and a voice shouted out "Praise Jesus!" Some slapped each other on the back and pointed at the figure on the stage, still not quite able to believe what they had just seen.

Waldo took McCrory by the hand and pumped his arm before he led him forward to show him to the audience. The applause grew to a roar, and people sprang to their feet.

"What do you think of magic now, Mr. McCrory? Do you still think this is some kind of trick?"

"No, sir!" He slapped his leg and danced a little jig. "This isn't no trick. It's a miracle. This here is my leg, just like it wasn't ever gone. I don't know how you did it, Mister, but you did it. You gave me my leg back. You gave me my life back."

" It was not I, Mr. McCrory. I was only the instrument. You must thank these good people for believing it could be done, and you must thank the power that has come down to me through the centuries."

Joseph Calendar knew that magic did exist, but still he wondered how the Amazing Waldo had transformed plastic into flesh and bone.

CHAPTER 28

Never once in his life had the very practical Arnold Acker considered the possibility that there might be unseen forces at work in the world. The evil that was done was carried out by men and women usually as ordinary as those who delivered his mail or showed him to a seat in the movie theatre. But when Dr. Malcolm Mills came to his office to tell him that he couldn't find any evidence in either of the murders beyond the theory that someone had probably smothered the life out of both Calpurnia Waters and J. C. Alphonse, he had to wonder.

"Nothing, Doc?"

"Well, there are signs of asphyxia in the lungs and throat, but I didn't find any bruising around the mouth and nose like you'd expect if somebody pressed a pillow over their faces. They both had traces of whiskey in their stomachs."

"Enough to knock them out so they couldn't resist?"

"I don't think so. It's as though each of them decided to simply lie down and stop breathing."

"So you don't have anything to show how they were murdered, then?"

"Murder by suffocation just isn't always easy to prove."

With his index finger, Acker pushed his fedora back on his head. Two people dead, and nothing to link them to their killer. The sergeant was more than halfway regretting that Nell Marchand had involved him in this particular case. He didn't have a clue what to tell her or her cook Hattie about what happened to her friend.

"All right, then, Doc. I reckon we'll have to keep looking. Thanks for coming all the way up here."

"I'll call a friend up in the New York examiner's office and ask him if they got any new tests I can try. I'd sure like to figure this out, but I'm not holding my breath. Ha. Holding my breath." The doctor hauled himself out of his chair. "I'm going home to get some sleep."

"Sounds like a good idea. Holler if you come up with something."

"You'll be the first one I call. If we don't figure it out, though, I just might call Ripley's Believe It or Not instead."

At the door, Dr. Mills saluted, clapped his hat on his head, and wandered out humming.

The sergeant chuckled. Police had their own gallows humor. He'd never known a medical examiner who didn't have a sense of humor, too. Had to, if he wanted to stay sane on the job. Otherwise, dealing with death every day might eat away at him. You had to find a way to take it all in stride.

Meanwhile, Acker had better be figuring out what to say to Nell Marchand. He'd found out in the Evans case that she was not a woman who liked being told there were no answers, and that was for a girl she'd never even laid eyes on before. Where her cook was concerned, he figured she'd be at least twice as hard to handle.

"MISS NELL, THAT POLICE SERGEANT IS AT THE DOOR," JENKINS SAID.

She put down the magazine she'd been reading.

"Thank you, Jenkins. Please tell him I'll be right there." She went to the kitchen in search of Hattie. "Sergeant Acker is here. You ready, or you want me to talk to him first?"

"No. I want to hear it myself. Might be good news. Might be he knows what happened to Calpurnia."

"I hope so, Hattie. I sure hope so."

CHAPTER 29

In her dressing room before the midday service at the Tabernacle, Sister Louise paced like a man waiting to be called for his date with the electric chair.

"How could that charlatan heal a man whom I could not . . . whom Jesus could not heal? Magic, my eye. Lord, we have had nothing but disaster since the moment that so-called magician set foot in Memphis."

She flopped down at her dressing table, looked at herself in the mirror, and pulled back the skin on her face for a brief reminder of the good looks that had been hers in her youth. Those looks and her stature had been at least part of what had drawn the throngs to her revivals. She still had an imposing figure, but when she released her skin again, the face that stared back at her looked worn out. Haggard. Decrepit.

"I'm getting old, Henry."

"You're just tired, Sister," her secretary said. "There is no woman more distinguished in all of Memphis. You've been working too hard. I wish you would let me book a vacation for you. Perhaps a week in Florida? The sun and rest would do you good, restore the roses to your cheeks."

Distinguished. That's what men said when they couldn't think of anything else to say to aging women. Even Henry saw it. Lord Almighty. She couldn't remember ever being this tired before in all her life. A week to restore her weary soul. Louise was tempted.

If she could sleep and rest, she could think again. Maybe he was right. She should take some time away. If a week was good, a month

111

would be better. Maybe she could get an ocean-view suite at the Breakers. Henry could manage the Tabernacle while she was in Florida. Whether he would admit it or not, she knew he was itching to put on a white robe and preach. And why not? He'd been with her long enough to know how God's work should be done.

"Henry, you always know what's best for me."

"Thank you, Sister. Whatever I can do to support you in your mission, you know I am prepared."

"How would you feel about taking over the sermons for a while?"

"Taking over?" The boy looked genuinely confused.

"Not just helping me write them, but preaching yourself."

The look on his face erased any lingering doubt Louise had. "Sister, I . . . you know I . . . if you ever . . . ." He wound down, and she couldn't help smiling.

"What I'm saying is that you're right, Henry. I'm tired. Threadbare down to my soul. I want to be by myself for a while, to think about what work the Lord is calling me to do next. Maybe it's time to leave the Tabernacle, go back to preaching to the poor, to doing true mission work. Lord knows there are more and more people who need help in this Depression. Who knows? I might even go to China. I hear they need missionaries there."

"But Sister—"

"It's not wrong to be ambitious, son, as long as you're ambitious for the Lord. You're ready. I wouldn't consider being away from the Tabernacle for even a minute if I didn't think you were. You already run our business. Now, it's time for you to lead the Lord's people along the path of righteousness."

"If you're sure, Sister."

"I'm sure, Henry. Very sure. You know, ever since I failed to restore that man's leg, I've doubted my gifts. You know what they say, the Lord giveth, and the Lord taketh away. Maybe that was a sign from Him that it's time for me to renew my faith with humbler work. Perhaps in my pride, I overreached myself."

She looked up in time to see a tear slide down her secretary's cheek before he could wipe it away. "Oh, my dear boy." She went to him and enfolded him in her arms. "I've had my day and will again. But today is for you."

"I won't let you down, Sister."

She released him and patted his cheek. "I know you won't. Remember it's the Lord's work you're doing, not mine." She turned back to the mirror and straightened her robes. Perhaps she would take a robe or two with her to Florida, just in case she should be called on to preach. It would never do to be unprepared. "Henry, tomorrow morning, I want you to call the Breakers in Palm Beach and book me a room. Tell them I'll be there for a month and that I want a balcony that overlooks the beach. There's nothing like eating shellfish and sleeping with an ocean breeze coming in through the window."

Just then, Evelina, the stage manager, popped in to give Louise the five-minute call. "The choir is wrapping up with 'Take My Life and Let It Be.'"

"Thank you, Evelina. That's perfect. Ready, Henry?"

"Yes, Sister. Whatever needs do be done, I'm ready." The smile he gave her was saintly.

CHAPTER 30

"We got another one, Acker," Murphy said, leaning against the jamb of the sergeant's open door.

"Another what?" The sergeant looked up from the report he was working on.

Murphy took the chair in front of the desk, turned it around, and straddled it. "Another corpse behind the theatre."

"Dammit." Acker flung his pencil down so hard that it bounced across the room. "Colored?"

"No, sir. White man this time. And there doesn't seem to be anything wrong with this one."

"Same janitor find him?"

"Yes, and he quit right after." Murphy couldn't help grinning. "Said he'd rather starve than keep running up on dead folks."

"I'm not sure I wouldn't feel the same way." The sergeant got up. "It's not exactly my favorite part of the job. Let's go take a look."

THE MAN'S BODY LAY STRETCHED OUT ON ITS BACK, DRESSED IN A WHITE shirt and black pinstriped trousers. He looked to be about 50 and in fairly decent shape. The only odd thing about his attire was that his shoes were mismatched. Acker crouched beside the corpse and pointed at the right shoe, which was heavier than the right.

"What do you make of this, Doc?"

Dr. Mills rocked back on his heels and rested his elbows on his knees to steady himself. "I've seen a few of those, but never at the end of a healthy leg. That's a special shoe for prosthetic limbs . . . artificial legs. If you'll look at the bottom, you'll see that is has a special sole to keep it from slipping on slick surfaces."

"What's this old boy doing wearing a prosthetic shoe?"

The medical examiner shrugged. "Could have been a handout. If you're down and out, any shoe that fits is a good shoe. But if that's the case, this fella must have gotten a whole new set of clothes recently. What he's wearing isn't threadbare. Doesn't look like a hobo to me."

"Find a wallet?" Acker said.

The beat cop who had arrived first on the scene handed a wallet to the sergeant, who flipped it open. "Yes, sir," the patrolman said. "His identification says his name is Ted McCrory. He's a vet."

"Are you kidding, Doc?" Murphy said. He sidled around for a look at the corpse's face. "That's the one-legged cripple got cured over at the magic show the other night. Ain't you heard about it? The Amazing Waldo shut him up in that Egyptian mummy case of his. The fella goes in with a fake right leg but comes out with his real leg on again. I never seen anything like it."

"I never took you for the magic show type, Murphy," Acker said.

"Yeah, well, my new girl wanted to go, so I took her. Never seen anything like it."

"You already said that. So, you mean to tell me the Amazing Waldo can grow new legs for folks?"

"I don't know how he did it, Sarge. I just know this here McCrory came in all gimpy, limping along on a plastic leg. Then the magician makes him disappear, but he shows up at the back of the theatre and comes running up onto the stage, hollering that he's healed. Wasn't anybody in the place didn't just about fall out of their seats. I never seen anything–."

"Yeah, I heard. You never seen anything like it. I don't know how he did it either, but it doesn't look like Mr. McCrory got to enjoy that new leg very long. I guess it's about time we go talk to old Waldo again. Seems like everybody turning up dead hereabouts has something to do with that show of his. This makes three."

The sergeant straightened. "All right, Doc. You'll let me know what you find, right?"

"Bound to be part of the pattern. If he's like the other two, it will be asphyxiation."

CHAPTER 31

Long before Memphis police did so, Joseph Calendar concluded that the Amazing Waldo had nothing to do with the three murders.

In the cool of the evening, Calendar strolled with Nell in her back garden. She picked up the first leaves that were beginning to fall from the oaks, unconsciously bunching them into an attractive arrangement in her hands.

As soon as the news of Ted McCrory's murder broke, Calendar had called at the Marchand mansion to discuss his theories about the killings. The idea that the murderer was after handicapped Negros proving baseless with the death of a healthy white man, the only things the victims had in common was their presence at performances by the Amazing Waldo and their attendance at healing services at Louise Henslowe's church.

"What could have been Waldo's motive in killing any of them?" he said. "For them all to die immediately after having taken part in his performances could only make him seem culpable. Even Waldo Peterfreund does not kill for sport. And even he is not brazen enough to leave the bodies behind his own theatre.

"Especially in the case of Calpurnia, who disappeared from the fairgrounds at quite some distance from the Odeon, it must have been difficult to transport a corpse between the two without being seen. And Hattie herself can bear witness to the fact that Waldo was at his tent until well after the performance ended. I think—and your vision confirms it, Nell—that whoever took her spirited her away from the stage as soon as she dropped through the trapdoor. I believe he took her alive, and wherever he killed her must have been close to the theatre."

"That's half of downtown Memphis," Nell said.

"Including the Tabernacle of Light, which is only three blocks away."

"Joseph, I can't believe Louise Henslowe is involved with the murders. When she was first starting her faith healing, she used to come to our house. My grandmother, Mared Blayney, was her friend, and, I suppose, in many ways her guide. I remember Grandmother doing readings for her more than once, predicting that she was destined to achieve fame, which she did, of course. When Louise set out on the road, it was unheard of for a woman to become an itinerant preacher. I remember asking Grandmother why anyone would choose that life, and she said, 'Pippin, she wants to bring love to people, a Billy Sunday kind of love.'

"She traveled all over the country spreading that love, never preaching any of the guilt and fear that so many of the other evangelists did. Like Reverend Sunday, she preached a personal relationship with God. In the beginning, she slept in her car by the side of the road and ate cold food out of cans so she could save every penny for her church. She built it on that foundation of sacrifice.

"You should have seen the Tabernacle of Light in its heyday. If they couldn't get a seat inside, people stood on the street just hoping to hear the choir sing or catch a glimpse of her when she got up to preach.

"She put on theatrical performances to illustrate some of her lessons. Grandmother and I went to hear her once, and it was the most amazing show I have ever seen in all my life. I'm sure you've heard Billy Sunday on the radio, preaching up a storm or carrying on about how we should keep Prohibition. Well, he had nothing on her. There was a time when everyone knew about Sister Louise. Her name was in the paper more than the president's."

"Did your grandmother continue to advise her?"

"At first, Louise consulted my nain whenever she landed in

Memphis between travels. I'm not sure what happened, if they had a falling out, but one day she stopped coming. I know Mared Blayney would not have approved of her deceiving people, of pretending to heal them. Anyway, I haven't seen her since I was a teenager."

"Do you know her to be a fraud?" Calendar said.

"No, I have no proof of it. There were always doubters, of course, and some scathing stories in the press, but she had a reputation for miraculous cures. I think she even started a shrine of some sort at her tabernacle here to house the crutches of all the people she healed. I've not seen it myself, but I hear there are so many that she had to buy a warehouse to store them all."

"Did you ever meet anyone she restored?"

"There was a girl in my class in school who had a stutter so bad that you really couldn't understand a word she said. Her mother took her to see Sister Louise, and she stopped stuttering. Went on to be an actress in New York. Sister Louise used to invite her to give speeches when she travelled to New York."

Nell bent to pick up a particularly pretty russet leaf to add to her collection. "Don't you believe faith healing is possible?"

"It's not that. Whether it's faith or optimism or something else, the mind can wield amazing power over the body. I've seen it happen myself, known great healers in my time, but I've also known shameless frauds who prey on the weak and gullible."

Nell blushed and shook her head. "You know, when we first met, I thought that's what you did—prey on those people."

"And now?"

"I don't believe you would ever willingly harm anyone. You might tell them what they want to hear, but if it brings them comfort or hope, then I'm not sure it's wrong. And I don't think you take advantage of anyone. Besides, it would be the pot calling the tea kettle black now if I took exception to it."

"That is something, at least."

"Now, you're teasing me." She bumped him with her shoulder.

"You know perfectly well that my original reaction wasn't unreasonable. How could I know otherwise?"

"With your great power, it's a mystery that you didn't sense the forces at work in the universe. And you had your grandmother as an example. But none of that matters now. You know that there is more."

"Well, I have busted right up against it, that's for sure."

"I'm sorry your introduction couldn't be more gentle, but it took those first visions to persuade you."

"Kind of like the story of the mule and the 2 by 4?"

This time Calendar laughed. "They did get your attention in a similar way."

Nell stopped in front of him, the look in her remarkable emerald eyes so open and trusting that his heart somersaulted within his chest. "Thank goodness you were there. I don't know how I would have found my way through it all without you."

Fighting the impulse to tip up her chin and kiss her, he reached for her hand instead. "I will always be here."

"Thank you, Joseph. That means a great deal to me." Nell withdrew her hand gently and began to move toward the house. "Now, what makes you think Louise Henslowe is involved?"

"The police have focused on Waldo because the connection between him and the three victims is clear. What they have overlooked is that they all had also consulted Sister Louise in some way, but she was unable to heal them. You remember that Hattie told us that Calpurnia had gone to her and received no help. The young boy, J. C., attended one of her healing services in hopes that she would be able to cure his deafness. And just a few days ago, this latest victim, Ted McCrory, made a very public plea during one of her services to have his leg restored, an undertaking that she must have known was impossible but that she attempted anyway."

"Or she believes in miracles."

"That may be so, but nonetheless, she failed."

"Yet, the Amazing Waldo did give the man his leg somehow."

"So he would have us believe. So all the people there that night saw with their own eyes. I saw him do it myself. But that was an illusion of some kind. It must have been. Waldo may be highly skilled, but I am not aware that he has any supernatural powers."

"So, you think Louise was taking revenge on these people, that she killed them because she failed to heal them? Whatever she may be or have done, I find that hard to believe. And even if she did, why on earth would she leave them behind the theatre? Why wouldn't she want to hide the bodies?"

"Leaving them to be found is meant to send a message of some kind that must be for Waldo. A warning of some kind. When we unravel that meaning, we may have the key to who killed them."

"Another question for which we must find the answer." Nell glanced up at the sky. "You know, I believe it's threatening to rain. Let's go back in."

————

ENSCONCED IN HER SITTING ROOM AGAIN, NELL LOOKED OUT OVER the garden, where the wind now sent the leaves whirling and swooping across the lawn. The first drops peppered the windows. She turned to Calendar.

"Joseph, since I have these great powers, I think it's more than time to put them to use. I must do a reading and hope it brings a vision."

Calendar hesitated, seemed reluctant to speak. He looked into her eyes, and she felt herself drawn into his as she had been before. Mesmerized. For a scant moment, their souls seemed to touch. His fear and his need surged through her, and she felt them as her own. She wanted to step toward him, to take him in her arms and comfort him, tell him that all would be well.

Then, the connection broke, and having decided something, he heaved a profound sigh. "Very well. If it is the only way, then it must be done. When would you like to attempt a vision?"

"No time like right this minute. You're here, and Hattie's here. My sitting room worked before. I like to sleep with Grandmother's cards close at hand, so I'll fetch them from my bedside table upstairs. I think Hattie is in the kitchen. I'll call her on my way."

Behind Nell, the rain slashed down in a torrent.

CHAPTER 32

A few moments later, Nell, Calendar, and Hattie gathered at a small table beside the fire. Nell fanned the cards out before her and closed her eyes, envisioning first Calpurnia and then J. C. When she felt that her mind was sufficiently at peace, when she sensed nothing but the sounds of her heart beating and her lungs breathing in and out, she opened her eyes again.

Letting her hands hover over the fan of cards, she waited for one of them to signal her to choose it. They were all quiet.

"Hattie, are you concentrating on Calpurnia?"

"Can't think about anything else."

"Give me your hand." Nell reached over her left and grasped Hattie's right. She closed her eyes again and focused as completely on Calpurnia as she could. Gradually, she began to sense a warmth beneath her hand that grew stronger as she moved closer to the center of the fan. She opened her eyes.

At last, she felt the heat increase and focus over one card at the very apex. She pulled it from the spread and turned it over. The Eight of Pentacles inverted. Cunning. Intrigue. Voided ambition. Under the right circumstances, that could be anyone. She held the card between her palms, closing her eyes again and summoning every ounce of concentration that she had.

This time, the vision didn't come in a flash as each one before it had done. At first, everything was darkness and quiet. Then, like the slow spread of dawn in the morning sky, the light came.

She was under the stage again with Calpurnia struggling to keep up with the figure that moved just ahead of her and dragged her along by the elbow, supporting her in the semidarkness until she emerged at the back and could stand shakily upright.

"Where we going?" Calpurnia said.

"Not far," the voice said, the figure still turned half from her so that she couldn't make out the face or the form very clearly. All she could distinguish was a pale, flowing garment. Then a swoop as the figure put some kind of hood over her head.

"What—"

But her protest was cut off before she could ask what in the world he was doing. Then he picked her up and carried her out into the afternoon's now-dimmed light.

Then, Hattie was shaking her and calling her name. "Nell! Nell, honey!"

Nell opened her eyes to find herself lying on the floor by the table, Hattie kneeling at her side with Joseph beside her, his face so pale that even his lips had gone white and his sapphire eyes shone like beacons.

"Lord, have mercy, Nell," Hattie said. "You like to scared us half to death. I been shaking you and hollering your name for the last five minutes. I was just about to send Dr. Calendar to call the ambulance."

Nell sat up and would have risen but realized that she couldn't get her legs to work right. Stretched before her at odd angles as though lifeless, they refused to respond. "Y'all help me over to the sofa, please."

Hattie started to pull up on one of Nell's arms, but Joseph pushed her aside and scooped Nell up. He carried her to the sofa and laid her on it as tenderly as a mother putting a sleeping child to bed. She shivered. He pulled the coverlet from the back of the sofa and spread it over her. When she tried to sit up, he put a restraining hand on her shoulder.

"Lie back, Nell, until you're sure you feel quite yourself. Are you cold?"

She nodded, shivering more violently still.

"Here, I'll get a fire going. Hattie, call for Jenkins and ask him to bring in some more wood."

"You think we need to call Dr. Roberts?"

Joseph leaned in close to Nell, rested his hand on her forehead and then alongside her cheek. "No. She's going to be all right. She's had an extremely intense vision, but she'll be fine as soon as we get her warm."

The cook popped out the door and back in. She took up a spot beside Nell, tucking the cover up under her chin.

The feeling began to return to Nell's limbs, starting as a tingling in her toes that spread gradually upward until she could feel her legs all the way up to her hips. Gingerly, she rotated each foot, relieved when it obeyed.

Jenkins raced in with an armload of wood from the pile by the kitchen door, and Joseph laid two more logs on the blaze that he had going in the fireplace. The driver and the medium came to stand over her, their faces anxious.

"Y'all stop staring at me." Nell sat up, pushing away Hattie's hand when she tried to hold her down. "You don't need to fuss over me."

Joseph's smile of relief held so much raw emotion that Nell had to look away from him for a moment. When she glanced at him again, he had composed his features into his customary air of calm amusement.

"I believe Miss Nell is all right, Hattie," he said. "Would you fix her a cup of tea, please?"

"And bring me a cold biscuit, too, please."

Hattie laughed. "I know this girl is all right if she wants to eat. Only time she's not thinking about food is when she's eating. I'll be right back, baby."

"Jenkins, don't you have something you need to be doing like polishing the Duesenberg?" Nell said.

"Yes, ma'am. You think this is enough firewood for now, Dr. Calendar, or would you like me to fetch another armload before I get back to work?"

"The flame is coming along nicely, and those other logs should be sufficient. If we need more, I can bring it in."

"No, sir. You need some more wood, you just holler. I'll be working in the kitchen 'til this storm lets up, and it won't take me two shakes to bring in as many logs from the back porch as you like. You stay here with Miss Nell."

Nell started to retort that she wasn't a child who needed tending, but she considered the worry on Jenkins's face. She held out her hand to him, and after a moment of hesitation, he took it. "Thank you, Jenkins. What would any of us do without you?"

Jenkins blushed. "Yes, ma'am. Well, I'd better get on back to the kitchen. That silver Hattie has me polishing is not going to shine itself up."

"What exactly happened?" she said to Calendar.

"You cried out in a terrible voice as though someone had run you through or ripped one of your limbs from its socket. Then you tumbled to the floor. You were so still and pale that I thought . . . ." Joseph paused, his throat working. That raw look flashed over his face again, and the struggle to compose himself again was clearer. "I feared for a moment that you were dead."

"I'm all right." She drew the coverlet up under her chin. "Just cold. So cold." Her teeth chattered.

"That should pass." Still, he rose and lifted another stick onto the fire. "Can you remember what you saw?" he said, resuming his place at her side.

"Calpurnia was under the stage again, but this time it was a continuation of what I saw before, of the first vision I had with Hattie. Whoever it was that was with her dropped a hood over her head and carried her off. Next thing I knew, I was waking up on the floor."

Hattie came in with a cup of tea, two biscuits that she had split open and toasted and spread with butter, and two healthy dollops of blackberry preserves.

Nell grabbed one of the biscuit halves, smeared it with preserves, and popped it into her mouth, whole. She washed it down with a gulp of good, strong, hot tea that Hattie had laced with plenty of sugar and cream, just the way she knew Nell liked it.

Smiling up at the cook, she picked up another biscuit half. "That's better. Thank you, Hattie." This time, she bit it in two and chewed slowly.

"Can I get you anything, Dr. Calendar?" Hattie said.

"Thank you, but I think I'll make do with a couple of fingers of Miss Nell's fine brandy. I can serve myself."

"Yes, sir. You need anything else, honey?"

"No, thank you," Nell said. "This is just exactly what I wanted."

"All right, then. You need me, I'll be in the kitchen figuring on what we can have for supper. You're staying, Dr. Calendar." It was a command, not question. "Anything special you'd like me to fix?"

"Hattie, whatever you prepare, I know it will be sublime. I leave myself in your hands."

She grinned at him and bustled off.

Calendar poured the brandy he had promised himself and sat beside Nell again. They were silent until she had finished the last bite of biscuit and the final drop of tea.

"Joseph, there was a darkness to this vision, an overpowering evil. And why would I faint? That has never happened before."

He swirled the brandy in his glass. "It's what I feared, Nell. The experience was more intense, more sinister, if you will. There is more at work here than you were prepared for."

"Perhaps you're right. The first visions terrified me, of course, because I didn't know what they were. I thought I was losing my mind. But while I was in them, I didn't feel anything beyond what Ginny was feeling. This time—" Although she was no longer cold, Nell shivered violently again. "This time, I felt a menace directed at Calpurnia and again at me."

"All the more reason we must consider our next move very carefully, Nell. I would not risk another vision, at least not until we know more. Not until I can think of a way we can protect you."

"All right, Joseph. No more visions for now. But at least we're closer. I'm sure the killer is a man. And he was wearing some kind of robe. We can't give up."

"No giving up. Those poor souls deserve justice. I intend to see that it is done, but it is no longer enough for you simply to consult me. I must take the lead here. Agreed?"

"Yes. All right."

That Joseph Calendar was afraid for her terrified Nell . . . and somehow made her feel safe for the first time in a very, very long time.

CHAPTER 33

In Waldo Peterfreund's suite at the Peabody, the magician's young assistant had run out of patience.

"Penelope, darling, I've told you a dozen times at least that you simply wave the vermouth over the gin. And add three olives. That's the way to make a proper martini."

Penelope darling wondered what had made her believe that being the Amazing Waldo's assistant would be all glamor, adulation, and exotic locales. So far, she was nothing but a drudge. Waldo expected her not only to deal with the theatre managers about their take of the house but to tote his tuxes to the cleaners, buy his gin for him, mix that gin into martinis that all tasted the same to her—like swill—and then climb into his bed at night. When he had first put his hand on her backside, she had told him in no uncertain terms that sleeping with him was not in her contract and that if he wanted someone to keep him warm, he could curl up with his cat Stinkmet or whatever her name was. Penelope was sure that was why Waldo—he had long since stopped being the Amazing anything to her—had been picking on her ever since.

Now, his martini wasn't right. Again. She was through with all this mess. He could learn to fend for himself, the overgrown, spoiled brat.

"You know, Waldo, if my mama hadn't brought me up to be a lady, I would tell you just what you could do with your extra olives. From now on, you can fix your own dadgum martinis. I'm not your maid or secretary or bartender. I signed on to be your assistant, period. If that

129

doesn't suit you, then you can just find another girl to put on these ridiculous outfits."

"Now, now, my dear. There's no need to be peevish. Had I realized that you found these little services so distasteful, I would never have asked you to do them for me. Matilda was with me for 10 years, and I never heard so much as a peep of complaint from her."

That was it. She'd rather go back to being a teller at the bank. The manager might be an old grump, but at least he didn't expect her to pick up his dadgum laundry. Penelope came to stand in front of Waldo, hands on her hips. "Well, then you'd better find good old Matilda and get down on your hands and knees to beg her to come back. As of right this minute, I am no longer your anything."

She marched into the room of Waldo's suite that was hers, grabbed her suitcase from under the bed, and stuffed the two dresses and nightgown that she had brought with her into it. All the clothes Waldo had bought her—which weren't much, if you thought about what he had promised her—she left behind. Let him pawn them off on the next girl fool enough to fall for his line. Her mama would say they were tacky anyway.

Marching through the living room of the suite, Penelope did not so much as look at Waldo.

Had she done so, the expression of rage on his face might have frightened her. He should never have let Matilda go without a fight. Breaking in new assistants was so tiresome. But most of all, Waldo did not like to be abandoned.

CHAPTER 34

At the Odeon, the Amazing Waldo was in his dressing room, warming up for the matinee performance when he caught sight in his mirror of Joseph Calendar watching him from the doorway. "I wondered how long it would before you came to see me," he said without turning around.

"How did you know I was here?"

"I always know where you are."

"You planning to hang around Memphis forever?"

Now, Waldo faced Calendar. "You know, I just might. Especially since I know it wouldn't suit you at all."

"How much longer do we have to keep doing this?"

"That's up to you, you know. It always has been. You know what I've always wanted."

"She isn't mine to give. Never has been. She always chooses freely."

"She's here, isn't she? In Memphis?"

Calendar didn't answer, but that was all the answer he needed.

"You know, I think it's time I pay her a social call. I've been meaning to, but with the police lurking about, it didn't seem proper somehow."

"Leave her alone, Nebi. Hasn't it been long enough?"

"It will never be long enough. Not until she's mine. You haven't called me Nebi for centuries."

"I'm asking you to remember how much you made her suffer. Isn't it enough yet?"

"What about my suffering? Doesn't that count for something? You started all this when you took her from me."

131

Calendar didn't respond.

"Does she know?" Waldo said.

"You know I'm not going to answer that."

"Ah, so she doesn't. At least not yet. Shall I tell her for you this time?"

"That won't change anything."

"I won't know until I try."

Calendar sat down wearily. "I'm not here to talk to you about Tadinanefer."

"So, this is a social call. I'm touched."

"I know you're not killing them."

"Killing whom?"

"The young Negress with polio. The deaf boy. The man with one leg. Do you know who's doing it?"

"Would you believe me if I said no?"

"Probably not."

"Then why ask?"

"Because their deaths are hurting people I care about."

Waldo turned back to his mirror. "You always did have a soft heart. That's why you couldn't learn the magic arts. You weren't willing to sacrifice for them."

"The price was too high."

"The price of power is always great. You're still playing at the great healer, aren't you?"

"It's my calling."

"I never could stand that about you, always acting the ever-virtuous acolyte. No wonder Imhotep chose you to take his place. He recognized his own weakness in you. It was my strength that threatened him, my strength that he hated."

"When you decided to become a follower of Seth and pursued the dark arts, he had no choice but to turn away from you. You know, once he told me that you were the most brilliant student he had ever had. It broke his heart to lose you."

Waldo snorted. "Tell me something, has your virtue made you rich?"

"I am comfortable."

"And what buys you that comfort? Lying to the weak and the gullible? How are you different from me? At least I confess my lies in the open. I just call them illusions. They have made me quite, quite wealthy."

Now, Calendar smiled at him. "Again, the price you pay is too great."

"This is growing tiresome. If you've had your say, run along. I have a show to prepare for."

For a long time after Calendar had pulled the dressing-room door quietly to behind him, Waldo sat staring at it in the mirror. At last, he shrugged, picked up his cape, and swung it around his shoulders.

Show time.

CHAPTER 35

Arnold Acker understood that the Memphis morgue needed to be cold, but he tried never to let himself think too carefully about why. He usually gave it a wide berth, but when the medical examiner called him to tell him that he had something interesting to show him about the latest corpse, Acker had to enter his domain.

Now the police sergeant leaned over Ted McCrory's body at the doctor's shoulder, the bitter, suffocating stink of formaldehyde sharp in his nose.

"You see these abrasions here?" the Dr. Mills said, pointing to the area around McCrory's knee. "And down here around the ankle?"

Glad to have something other than the Y-incision in the corpse's torso to concentrate on, Acker leaned in closer. There was a ring of chafing around the dead man's knee and just above the ankle. "Yeah, Doc. What's the verdict?"

"Any guess what caused these?"

"Nary a one." It was a game Dr. Mills liked to play sometimes, telling the police just enough to let them guess what the cause of injury or death might have been. But Acker couldn't figure out how some cuts around some fella's ankle could have killed him. "What do you think did it, Doc?"

"Well, now, I had to ponder on that for a while. But then I got to thinking about how that magician claimed to have restored this old boy's leg, and I took another look at it. Then I called my brother-in-law over at Memphis Prosthetics and Limbs and asked him to send me over some of the artificial legs they had in stock."

The doctor reached behind Acker to the table beside the gurney on which lay Ted McCrory's remains and picked up what looked to the sergeant like a long, pink cylinder. "This here is one of the new all-plastic models that's supposed to look more like a real human leg."

"All right, Doc, what's that got to do with McCrory here?"

The doctor held the artificial leg over the corpse's right one. "Notice anything?"

Acker peered and scrutinized, but for the life of him, he couldn't figure out what the doc wanted him to see. "Nope."

The medical examiner snorted in disgust. "Now, you're just being as contrary as a Mississippi mule. Look here." He jabbed a finger in the direction of the legs.

Acker squinted down at the limbs, fake and flesh. The top of the fake one reached to the corpse's knee, and the bottom hit him right at his ankle. "Well, I'll be damned."

"That's right. It's a good fit, isn't it? I believe Mr. McCrory here passed himself off as an amputee by sawing one of these plastic limbs in two and then fitting it over his own leg. That's what the chafing is—where the artificial leg rubbed against the skin beneath. These prosthetics weren't intended to be worn over existing limbs. They were made to take their place. Every time McCrory took a step on it, the plastic must have dug into his own leg."

"Why on earth would he want to pass himself off as a cripple?"

"It would be very handy for the performing of miracles if you could appear to restore your leg by removing the false one that covered it."

"So, that's how the Amazing Waldo cured him."

"Exactly."

"Well, I'll be damned," Acker said again. "That could work out to be a nice little racket."

"Except that you couldn't perform the cure too often. Sooner or later, it's going to get in the paper or someone figures it out. The way I see it, this was a one-time thing. There's no evidence of older abrasions on McCrory's leg or any wounds on his left one. Our dead man here never had a chance to try his trick more than once."

Acker scratched his head. This was an interesting development that he would have to take up with the magician during their next interview. Waldo Peterfreund could have killed McCrory to keep him from revealing the hoax. It was a plausible motive.

"Thanks, Doc. I owe you a cup of coffee for this one."

"How about a catfish dinner at the One Minute instead?"

"You got it. Name your day. Meanwhile, I think I'll swing by the station and get Murphy so we can make a little call on the Amazing Waldo. This time, I think I'll take along my handcuffs."

CHAPTER 36

This business with the Memphis police and everyone else asking him questions was growing most irksome. First the little round Irish cop and the tall one with the face like a sad hound dog had come around, all but accusing him openly of killing those unfortunates. Could he help it if they had chosen to arrive at his show just before their deaths?

At least Joseph Calendar, despite having some experience of what it was like to cross him, had realized that he hadn't done it. Now the police were back again, Murphy and Acker, asking him about Ted McCrory and the miraculous healing of the leg. He should have known better than to let McCrory draw him into his scheme. The man was obviously a grifter, but the idea of the Miracle of the Leg had been too good to resist.

And even better because it allowed him to beard that pious, priggish priestess, Sister Louise Henslowe, who had been preaching against the evils of magic and referring to him as the Devil's own minion again. He wasn't sure she had accepted his invitation to attend the performance that night, but the story of the cure, of McCrory leaping up on the stage as lightly as Nijinsky, must have reached her. He had no doubt that his miracle had put her in her place most satisfactorily.

So, he had paid McCrory and thought him well worth the price. But now the whole thing was blowing up in his face. No, he never should have given in to the temptation to show Sister Louise up.

Acker and Murphy sat across from him in the living room of his suite, the sergeant asking the questions, and the officer taking the notes.

"Today, I had a very interesting visit with Dr. Mills, our medical examiner, and your buddy Ted McCrory," Acker said.

"Really?" Waldo said, feigning a polite interest.

"It was the damnedest thing." The sergeant paused and exchanged the kind of look with Murphy that you give a friend when you're sharing a joke with him. "Seems like Mr. McCrory never did have an artificial leg at all. He just covered his own leg up with this plastic one so folks would think he was cripple, but all the time, there wasn't anything wrong with him at all. Nothing at all. He was as fit as you or Murphy here."

Acker and Murphy shared a grin again. It was really becoming quite obnoxious.

"Fascinating," Waldo said.

"Now, I just figured you'd think it was, Mr. Peterfreund. But I reckon you knew all about that leg beforehand, didn't you? Pretty neat trick, though, fooling all those folks in the audience into thinking you could perform a real, live miracle."

Waldo inclined his head, smiling. No use in going on with the charade. "It was one of my more memorable illusions."

"You sure had me going," Murphy said. "My eyes like to popped right out of my head when I saw him come running up the aisle like that. The lady next to me passed clean out and fell across two or three people on the other side. They had to carry her outside so she could get some air before they could get her to come to."

"I do like to engage my audience, Officer. It does my heart good to know that I succeeded so well."

"Yep, that was a great trick," Acker said. "I'm just sorry I wasn't there to see it myself. I don't reckon you'll have the chance to repeat it, Ted McCrory being dead and all."

"No. That is most unfortunate. Poor man. He was really quite clever, you know."

"You saying the whole thing was his idea?"

"I added some refinements—the pirouette onto the stage was my inspiration—but the original scheme was all his. As I said, quite clever."

"So, why'd you kill him?"

Waldo paused as though considering whether or not to confess to the heinous deed just to see what they'd do. Acker and Murphy both leaned forward in their seats expectantly. He really shouldn't enjoy baiting them so. "I'm sorry to disappoint you, gentlemen, but Mr. McCrory was quite alive when I last saw him."

"And when would that have been, Mr. Peterfreund?"

"Please call me Waldo, Sergeant. Mr. McCrory came by my dressing room right after the performance. I cautioned him not to spend his very liberal fee all in one place. We shared celebratory slugs of whiskey, and I bid him good evening."

"How much did your little miracle set you back?"

"A hundred dollars."

"Seems pretty cheap."

"Oh, it was, considering. He wanted half of the show's take for the night, but I persuaded him that a hundred dollars was a princely sum for which he should be grateful. I pointed out that I would probably recover from the scandal of being unmasked but that people were unlikely ever to forgive him for engaging their sympathy and then revealing that it had been so sadly misplaced. He seemed to grasp that. I wished him well, and he was on his way. Believe me, I was as downcast as anyone when I heard he was dead."

"Yes, I can see that you're just broke out with the milk of human kindness," Acker said.

"And just how did you hear about it, Peterfreund?" Murphy asked.

"I have my sources among the gentlemen of the press."

The officer's only response was to grunt and scribble more determinedly in his notebook. Waldo suspected that he had an idea who that source might be.

"Why should we take your word for it that McCrory was alive when you saw him?" Acker said.

"Sergeant, I never lie. I may practice a little deception in some of my illusions—it is, after all, part of my stock in trade—but I never tell an out-and-out lie, especially to the police. After all, what reason could I have to dispatch the poor, unfortunate Ted McCrory after he had rendered me such a great service?"

"Because he threatened to expose your trick, to discredit you. He was blackmailing you for more money, so you killed him to shut him up."

"A very colorful theory but, alas, quite mistaken. As I have explained, Mr. McCrory came to understand that he would have more to lose by revealing our little secret than would I. After we had discussed the possibility of what might happen if he did, he seemed quite content with the remuneration I offered him. I assure you, we parted ways the best of friends."

Murphy looked up from his notebook and grunted again.

"Your lack of faith in me is quite distressing, Officer Murphy. If you were, indeed, among the audience that night, you saw the effect our little performance had. People like to be astounded, to believe that miracles can happen. I imagine we both found our success in fulfilling those expectations quite gratifying. I know I did at least. I'm afraid you will have to look elsewhere for your killer."

Waldo made a great show of consulting his watch. "Now, if you will excuse me, gentlemen, I would like to have the remainder of the afternoon to rest for tonight's performance."

Acker and Murphy exchanged another glance, but there was no smirking now. Waldo seemed to have won his point and frustrated their efforts to get him to incriminate himself. He found himself feeling rather magnanimous toward them both. "If you like," he said, "I could arrange to leave tickets for you at the box office for this evening's show. Sergeant Acker? Officer Murphy? It would be my honor to have you as my guests."

Murphy looked as though he might be about to accept when Acker cut him off. "Thank you, Mr. Peterfreund, but that wouldn't be ethical. We can't go around accepting favors from murder suspects."

"Most unfortunate," Waldo said, making a small moue in Murphy's direction. "Perhaps when you have found the real murderer, you will do me the honor of enjoying my hospitality. Until then, gentlemen...." He walked to the door of his suite and held it open for the two policemen, who stepped out into the hallway.

"We'll be in touch, Mr. Peterfreund," Acker said.

"I have no doubt that you will, Sergeant Acker." Waldo closed the door behind him and went into his bedroom for a restorative nap. The exchange had proven rather draining, and he wanted to be at his best for the performance.

"WHAT DO YOU THINK, SARGE?" MURPHY ASKED ON THE WAY DOWN IN the elevator.

"He's one cool customer, I'll give him that."

The elevator reached the lobby of the Peabody, and Acker and Murphy stepped out. On the way past the lobby fountain where the Peabody ducks swam, Acker turned to Murphy. "You would have taken those tickets if I hadn't stopped you, wouldn't you?"

"You're damned right I would have." The way Murphy said it, it sounded like "wood uv." "The Amazing Waldo puts on a first-class show. You ought to catch it one night if you can. Take Mrs. Acker. I bet she'd eat it up with a spoon."

Acker smiled. Murphy made no secret of his crush on Marta. Maybe if they cleared Waldo, he would take her. He enjoyed a good show himself, and he'd never seen a magician perform before. If you were going to start somewhere, you might as well start at the top.

CHAPTER 37

The next morning when he read the headline on the front page of the Memphis Press-Scimitar, Arnold Acker was less taken with the conjurer. "Renowned Magician Reveals Hoax," the lead story read. It went on to say that the Amazing Waldo—who had recently taken up an extended run at the Odeon Theatre and was performing nightly to sell-out crowds—had shared with reporter Osgood Sherman that he had been deceived into believing he had accomplished a magic feat of such astonishing skill that it had bordered on a miracle in restoring the missing leg of an unfortunate veteran of the Great War who had come to him seeking help. The illusionist went on to abhor the deception that the man had perpetrated on the unsuspecting audience in only pretending to have lost his leg in service of his country. The Memphis police were believed to be in search of the man's confederates, who were, no doubt, responsible for his murder.

A photograph of the magician looking suave but contrite accompanied the article.

"Why, you sly son of a bitch," Acker muttered to himself over his morning coffee. "I didn't see that one coming."

"What did you say, sweetheart?" Marta said, bringing the coffee pot to refill his cup.

"Looks like our prime suspect just knocked the stuffing right out of one of our cases."

"The magician? I'm sorry."

"That's all right, dumplin'. If he did it, we'll catch him. He's just made it a little harder for us to find a jury when he goes to trial."

"And if he didn't do it?"

"Well, then, we'll keep looking 'til we find out who did." Acker scooted his chair back from the table and patted his knee. "Now, come here and give me a kiss."

Marta obliged, sitting on his lap and giving him the kind of sugar that made a good Southern man think that it wouldn't be a crime to be late for work just once in his life. He buried one hand in her hair and pulled her closer with his other arm.

"Your coffee's getting cold," she said.

"I bet there's another pot where that came from." He nuzzled her neck for good measure.

"Maybe so, but you'll have to make it yourself. It's one to a customer around here."

"My coffee's better than yours is anyway."

"Is that so?" Marta pulled away, pretending to be angry. "Then maybe I'll just let you fix it from now on."

"Long as you don't make me do any of the cooking, I'll be happy to make the coffee."

"That's a deal." She kissed him again.

Sergeant Acker did end up being late for work that morning. When they saw the smile on his face, no one at headquarters wondered why, especially Officer Murphy, who thought Arnold Acker was one lucky son of a gun.

THE POLICE SERGEANT WAS NOT THE ONLY ONE TO READ THE STORY IN the Press-Scimitar and reflect on what a wily and devious opponent Waldo Peterfreund was. Up town in his fashionable house in Central Gardens, Joseph Calendar had his confirmation that the magician was not Ted McCrory's killer. As daring as Waldo was, it seemed too risky a maneuver to taunt the police so openly if he were, indeed, guilty.

There was always the chance that he had killed Calpurnia Waters and J. C. Alphonse, but Calendar could see no benefit to Waldo in doing so. That doubt confused matters even more. After all, unlike the first two victims, McCrory was not actually handicapped. The papers had revealed that the first two bodies had been found behind the Odeon Theatre. A second killer could distract attention from himself by leaving McCrory there, too. And if Waldo was not the killer, what was the message or warning for the magician in leaving the corpses at the theatre? Unless there were another connection, a connection that he had not yet uncovered, he was as much in the dark as ever.

Meanwhile, Joseph Calendar discovered a grudging admiration for his old enemy's command of the principles of publicity. Going to the papers with the story of the Hoax of the Leg was a stroke of genius intended, no doubt, to replenish flagging audience numbers. A true stroke of genius.

CHAPTER 38

Sister Louise Henslowe was looking forward to her last sermon before she boarded the train to Palm Beach and a month of freedom. She loved the church and her congregation, but it was time to allow someone to relieve the load for her for a while at least.

Behind her, a knock came on her office door. "Come in, Henry."

But it was not Henry who came to stand at her desk, hat in hand. In fact, she didn't remember ever seeing the country-looking man somewhere in his forties who smiled confidently at her, a crooked front tooth protruding slightly from underneath his upper lip in a way that she found oddly charming. Still, the man had no business walking into her office without so much as a by your leave. Henry usually kept her followers from invading her inner sanctum. It was her place to reflect and prepare, and only a select few of her staff were allowed in it. She was about to call out for her secretary when the stranger spoke.

"Sister Louise, my name is Mordecai Jones, and I am the answer to your prayers."

At that, Louise found herself smiling back at him. So this was the preacher the Amazing Waldo had made so famous by supposedly accepting Christ at his altar. If Waldo had sent him, it behooved her to find out why. She sat back and gave him an appraising look. "Is that so, Mr. Jones? And which of my prayers have you come in answer to, may I ask?"

"It's Brother Jones, ma'am. I'm a minister, just like you. Got my own church over on the other side of town. The Church of the Redeemer's Blood. Maybe you heard of it."

"No, Brother Jones, I'm afraid I haven't." He seemed a little crestfallen at that. "But, then, you see, so much of my time is taken up with my work here at the Tabernacle of Light that I seldom have the opportunity to venture forth to other houses of worship. But how may I help you?"

"It's me that's come to help you, Sister."

"I see. And what form does that help take, Brother Jones?"

"I heard your talk on the radio Sunday night." He started to pull out the chair in front of her desk, stopped, and looked to her for permission. "All right if I sit down?"

His brazenness was beginning to amuse her. She would hear him out, this Mordecai Jones. "Please do."

"Anyway, like I said, I heard your program on the radio Sunday night, how you said you was going to a retreat down in Florida to rest and pray so you could continue the Lord's work. I know how that can wear you out, preaching, and you do it two times a day most days, don't you?"

Louise inclined her head and smiled.

"Anyway, I figured you might need somebody to come take over the preaching here at the Tabernacle. There been so many folks coming to hear me over at the Redeemer's Blood that we don't hardly have room for them anymore, so I thought we could—what do they call it?—join forces. Put our two churches together. I mean, the Tabernacle of Light is so big that you wouldn't hardly notice my congregation mingling in with the folks you already got here. And as I build my following, I figure there'd be room for everybody."

"That is an interesting proposal," Louise said. She watched Brother Jones, who smiled again, exposing that fascinating tooth. "Brother Mordecai—you don't mind if I call you by your first name, do you? Good. Brother Mordecai, I have already chosen from among the closest of my staff here at the Tabernacle to provide for the pastoral care of my congregation in my absence. Henry Barcroft has served me loyally for many years and helps me with my weekly radio sermons. Why should I choose a man unknown to me over a trusted lieutenant?"

Jones struggled for words for a moment before his eyes lit up. "Sister Louise, you're the reason I became a preacher. My mama and me went to hear you preach at the camp meeting over in Tiptonville where I grew up. That night, you brought me to Jesus, and I owe you everything I have done in my life since then. Why, if it hadn't been for you, I might have ended up a drunk dead in a ditch on the side of the road like my old daddy. Everything I know about preaching and the Gospel I know from listening to you on the radio. If you give me a chance, I know we can do good work together."

"That's quite flattering, Brother Mordecai."

"It's just the God's own truth, Sister."

She tapped her fingertips together to help her think. Perhaps it would be wise for Henry to keep an eye on Mordecai Jones and share his duties with someone who had more experience in actual preaching before a crowd. A time or two when she was indisposed, he had taken over her radio broadcast and done quite well. But he had yet to stand at the altar before the multitudes that could throng the Tabernacle and preach. Despite his connection with Waldo, there was something simple and solid about this man, something genuine that she felt she could trust. Henry might not like being asked to share the Tabernacle pulpit with anyone and most certainly not with Jones, but he would understand her reasoning and do what was best for the church. He always did.

"All right, Brother Mordecai," she said standing to offer him her hand. "I agree that there is strength in numbers. You and your flock are most welcome to join our family at the Tabernacle of Light. Let me introduce you to Henry, who will show you around and provide you with everything you need."

"Thank you, Sister. You won't ever regret this. I will do you proud."

"I'm sure you will, Brother. I'm sure you will." She smiled a little, wondering if anyone else would notice that it was going to take two men to replace her.

LOUISE HENSLOWE HAD BEEN RIGHT. THE IDEA OF SHARING THE PULPIT with Mordecai Jones did not please Henry at all. Devoted as he was to Sister Louise, he secretly thought her sometimes too soft. That she was willing to take in a turncoat like Jones was proof of it. Henry wanted to bring the Tabernacle of Light a style of preaching that reminded sinners that God wanted them to consider what the fires of Hell would feel like if they disappointed Him.

"Sister, forgive me, but what do we really know about this Mordecai Jones?" Henry said, pacing up and down before the window in her office. "I mean, he could be anyone. He could be pretending to be a man of God, someone the magician set up in that storefront to siphon off attention from your work here. Are you willing to unleash an unknown force on your followers?"

"Henry, sit down and stop that pacing. You're going to wear a hole in the carpet." She waited for him to take the chair before she continued. "How long have we worked together?"

"Ten years, Sister."

"And all that time, have you simply been waiting for me to die or retire so you could take over?"

If she had slapped him across the face, the boy could not have looked more thunderstruck. "Sister, I–"

"I didn't think so. You know I love you like a son. Especially in these last few years, I don't know how I would have made it through the hard times without you. When it was time to stop traveling to every revival and camp meeting that invited me, you helped me decide to come home to Memphis. Much of what I've achieved here at the Tabernacle is because I knew I could count on you to manage its affairs while I concentrated on the congregation's spiritual growth. We wouldn't be where we are today if it weren't for you."

"Thank you, Sister."

"Now, I want you to think about what I've just said. We've been a team. We're like the body and the soul of the church. You are the body, its strength, the heart that pumps the blood that keeps it going day to day. But what is the body without the soul?"

"Nothing," he said quietly. "Sister, are you saying that I lack the spirit to lead the Tabernacle? Why can't I be both?"

"No, what I'm saying is that I believe you and Brother Jones would make a good team, just as you and I have. I've asked around, and his little storefront church was there long before that charlatan the Amazing Waldo came to Memphis. Jones is a man of God, and he has now attracted quite a following. He has the experience that you lack as a spiritual leader. You have the business sense that he needs. More important than that, you have the polish and sophistication that he lacks. He makes no bones about coming from a poor farm family, and frankly, I believe his homespun appeal could be good for the Tabernacle. But he could use some of the refinement that you have. And you, my dear boy, could learn from him about being a man of the people. No one doubts that you are brilliant, Henry, but I'm afraid you can come across as a little cold to the less-educated among our flock. Do you understand what I'm trying to say?"

"Yes, Sister, I think I do."

Red splotches were emerging on Henry's cheeks as they did when he struggled to control some emotion that was about to overtake him. She had hurt him. Louise came around the desk, leaned against it beside him, and took both his hands in hers.

"You know I must think of what's best for the Tabernacle. And once Mordecai sees what it means to be part of our work here at the church, why any influence that so-called magician may still have over him is bound to fade."

The boy managed a sickly smile, and she released his hands.

"Now, I've had a similar talk with Brother Jones, though not about Waldo, of course. He says he's ready, as he put it, to be hitched in the same harness with you. Will you promise me that you'll do your best to work with him?"

"Yes, Sister Louise."

"Thank you. Now I can get on my train to Florida with my mind at ease. And if it doesn't work, if you can't pull together like two mules hitched to the same wagon, well, then, when I come back to Memphis, we'll decide how best to go on."

"If you think it's what we should do, Sister, then I will be guided by you, of course."

Louise watched him to see if he truly agreed or only pretended to do so to avoid upsetting her. He returned her gaze with an expression of forthright trust that assured her he accepted her will.

"You know, Henry, as soon as I met Mordecai, I saw that he was one of the rocks I could build my church on, just as Peter was for our Lord. The only other time I have felt that way was when I first met you. Do you remember that day?"

"As though it were yesterday."

"You staggered up to my altar wild and thin as a March mule. I thought I was going to have to cast out an evil spirit like Jesus at Capernaum."

"But then you put your hand on my head."

"Yes, and you quieted. Young as you were, I knew that the Lord had sent you to be my shield and my protector. That in healing you, I accepted a contract between us. When dear old Grace, rest her soul, couldn't carry on any more as my secretary, there was no one else I wanted as my right hand but you.

"Now, there were some on the church council who didn't want me to hire you. They said you were too young, that it wasn't proper for me to have a man in such an intimate and trusted position. But I relied on the Lord and my heart to guide me, and I have never regretted that for one moment."

"So, now I'm asking you to trust me. Make Mordecai Jones your ally. Together, I believe you can do great things. And when the day comes that I am ready to lay down my burden for good, I can do so in peace, knowing that I have entrusted my Tabernacle to Henry Barcroft and Mordecai Jones."

"Yes, Sister. I won't let you down."

Good. The boy spoke from his heart. Sister Louise kissed Henry on the cheek.

"Now, help me with my suitcase. I don't want to miss my train."

CHAPTER 39

The one thing that Sister Louise had not discussed with her two replacements was who should take over the Friday evening healing services. Perhaps she had assumed that no one would continue them at the Tabernacle until her return. But when Friday morning rolled around and Evelina asked Henry if she should have the men set up the stage as usual, he said yes.

Over the years, he had certainly watched Sister perform enough healings that he knew how he should proceed. If the Lord chose to work through him, then he could prove to her that he was more than just the body of the church. He had agreed to let Brother Mordecai take the pulpit for this first Sunday since Sister Louise had boarded her train, so he had no qualms about not discussing the Friday evening service with him.

That evening he waited in the wings for the song leader and choir to get the congregation into a properly receptive frame of mind. There was nothing like singing at the top of your lungs to bring you closer to heaven, Sister always said.

"Got a pretty good crowd tonight," Evelina whispered to him. "You nervous?'

"No," Henry said. "Well, maybe a little. But I prayed this afternoon and offered myself up to the Lord as His instrument. It's up to Him whether He chooses to use me or not."

"Amen," the stage manager said.

They waited for the choir to file out into the sanctuary to take their places among the congregation. It was important for the flock to feel that they were all part of one family.

Evelina patted him on the back and gave him a gentle push toward the stage. "All right. You're on. Good luck, Henry."

He had never realized how bright the lights on the stage were. He climbed up to the pulpit to deliver his homily. A catalogue of the Savior's healing miracles seemed appropriate to set the scene. The rapt attention on the faces of his audience encouraged him and lifted him up. By the time he took his place at the altar, Henry felt that he was all but floating above himself, looking down at what he was doing.

"Brothers and sisters," he said, "in her absence, Sister Louise has entrusted your wellbeing to me. If there are those among you who suffer illness or who have known affliction, I invite you to come forward now for healing. Offer your trouble up to the Lord. Ask Him to forgive your sins. Pray with me, and we will ask Him to make you whole."

Eyes scanning the congregation, he waited. He felt himself full of the Spirit, but what if no one came? "Will no one come and ask the Lord to take away his suffering?"

Toward the front, a man so white with age that that his skin was translucent rose from his seat and hobbled toward the altar. Henry marveled that he could breathe, let along walk. Henry nodded at Evelina, who sent two of her robed stagehands down to help him up the steps.

"Tell me your burden, brother, so that I may ask the Lord to lift it from you." Henry said when the man had reached him. He held the microphone toward him so the congregation could hear his answer.

"I got the cancer, the doctors tell me. My first great-grandchild is coming in January. If the Lord can let me live to see him, then I can go on to Glory happy."

Normally, Henry would have asked the old man to kneel with him, but in deference to his age, they would remain standing. "Where is the cancer?"

"Here, in my lung." The old man placed his hand over his right ribcage.

"What is your name, brother?"

"Abner. Abner Wallace."

Henry laid his hands on either side of the man's chest, closed his eyes, and lifted his face. "Oh Lord Jesus who has made the dead rise and the blind see, look down on this Your child Abner who comes to You seeking to be whole. Reach out Your hand and take the cancer from his lung. If it be Your will, return to him his health."

Not sure whether he should sense something, whether his hands should grow warm or he should feel the power flowing through him, Henry waited. When at last the old man coughed, Henry released him and stepped back.

"How do you feel, brother? Did you experience the Spirit moving within you?"

The old man smiled beatifically at him. "Yes, Brother Henry, I believe I did." He drew a deep lungful of air. "Been a good while since I could get my breath right. It's a blessing to be able to do it again."

"Then, praise the Lord. Go forth and enjoy your time with your family."

It took the stagehands a while to escort Abner to his family, who embraced him, weeping.

While he waited, Henry scanned the congregation, smiling encouragement. "Who else will come?"

Now, a simple country woman came forward, leading a teenage girl who looked frightened and sadder than anyone he had ever seen before in his life.

When they reached the altar, the girl pulled back for a moment, shaking her head and turning away.

"It's all right, Gladys," the woman said. "Let Brother Henry help you."

Henry held out his arms to summon them, and the two made their way onto the stage to take their places beside him. He held the microphone out toward the girl. "What is your affliction, child?"

"She can't talk, Brother Henry," the woman said, pulling the microphone to her own mouth. "Never has said a word since she was three."

"Can your daughter hear?"

"She ain't my daughter. She's my granddaughter, and she can hear good as you and me. Her mama run off when she was three and left me and her poppa to raise her up best we could. Last spring, he took the fever and died. We come into town looking for work. I got me a job down at the Peabody, cleaning rooms. They let Gladys here help me, but don't nobody want to hire a girl that can't talk." On her tongue, "hire" sounded like "har" and "can't" became "cain't."

"And she has never spoken since?"

"Not since she was a little bitty thing."

Henry placed his hands on either side of the girl's face and pressed gently. When she started to pull her face from his hands, he smiled at her. "It's all right, Gladys. I won't hurt you. Put yourself in the Lord's hands."

She grew still, wide-eyed but looking less frightened and despondent.

"Lord," Henry said, "this is Your child, Gladys. Heal her that she may find her voice to praise You."

This time, Henry's arms and hands tingled so that he was sure Gladys must feel it, too. He began to sweat with the effort of the Spirit flowing through him and into her. Then, his hands sprang apart of their own volition, and he staggered back. "Hallelujah!" he said.

"Hallelujah," Gladys said, softly. "Hallelujah," she repeated, and her voice rang out through the sanctuary, strong and true. Tears spilled past her lashes and down her face, but her smile was that of a slave greeting her first day of freedom.

Her grandmother fell to her knees at the preacher's feet and kissed his hand.

He took her by the elbows and lifted her to her feet. "Get up, sister," he said. "Thank the Lord, not me. I am only His instrument."

Henry stretched his arms over the congregation. "Hallelujah!"

"Hallelujah!" they shouted back.

He wished Sister Louise could have been there to see it.

THE AMAZING WALDO SAT AT THE BACK OF THE SANCTUARY, SMILING. Knowing that her minion had accomplished what she had not been able to do would irk Louise Henslowe.

AFTER THE SERVICE, EVELINA AND THE LIGHTING MAN WERE TALKING over where to reposition the spotlights for Sunday morning.

"You had me worried, adding that girl like that," he said. "I had to scramble to get the spot on her in time. I thought we were going to start slow, just do the old man. Got to hand it to you, though. The girl was good. Had the congregation eating right out of Henry's hand. Where'd you find her?"

"I've never laid eyes on that girl or her granny before in my life."

CHAPTER 40

When next she saw Waldo Peterfreund, Nell was at lunch with Bess Marchand. Her mother-in-law had a particular weakness for the chicken salad at the Arcade Restaurant downtown on South Main Street, and Nell treated her to it at least once a week. That morning, she and Bess had gone shopping at Lowenstein's for foundation garments, as Bess liked to call them. Jenkins loaded the discretely wrapped packages into the Duesenberg, and Nell asked him to stop back for them in an hour and a half.

They had just settled at a table near the front when the owner, Speros Zepatos, came out to greet them and flirt with Bess, who had been coming to the restaurant since the day he opened its first incarnation in 1919.

"Miss Bess, you grow more beautiful every day," he said. "Why don't you run away with me?"

"I'm not sure your family would approve, Mr. Speros."

Zepatos twinkled at her. "Oh, they all have their own lives. They won't notice what happens to an old man like me."

Bess giggled like an ingénue. It was always the same. Mr. Zepatos asked her to run away with him, she blushed, and then he went to the kitchen to prepare their lunches himself.

"I swear, Mother, one of these days you ought to take Mr. Speros up on his offer just to see what he would do."

The old lady giggled again. "Now, Nell, you know he's only being gallant. He wouldn't a bit more run away with me than a hoot owl. I

157

bet he carries on like that with all the ladies. The Greeks are naturally charming."

"Well, you might get a free trip to Greece out of it. Wouldn't that make the ladies in your bridge club pea green with envy?"

Bess Marchand pursed her lips into a very proper little smile and shook her head, but she blushed again. Nell was positive she was at least considering the possibilities. Bess and her late husband the Judge had been devoted to each other, but Nell had seen her notice a handsome face more than once. Her mother-in-law might be old, as the saying went, but she wasn't dead.

They were just digging into dishes of peach ice cream that Mr. Speros insisted were on the house when Nell felt a chill that she couldn't blame on eating hers too fast. She looked up to find the magician standing over her, that same intense look in his eyes that had paralyzed her at Calpurnia's funeral. She couldn't smother the gasp that escaped her.

"Forgive me, ladies," he said, bowing first to her and then to Bess, "I didn't mean to startle you." He turned his gaze on Nell again. "When I saw you at that poor unfortunate's funeral, I couldn't help feeling that we have met before."

Sitting as far against the back of her chair as she could manage, she didn't answer.

Her Southern hostess instincts robust and deeply ingrained, Bess began to glance anxiously from her to Waldo and back again. "I am Bess Marchand," she said at last, unable to endure what no doubt seemed to her to be a shameful lack of manners on Nell's part. "This is my daughter-in-law, Nell Marchand." She offered Waldo her hand. "May I know your name, sir?"

"Mother," Nell said, a note of warning in her voice. Bess ignored her.

"I am Waldo Peterfreund, otherwise known as the Amazing Waldo, Miss Bess." He leaned over her hand like an Old World count.

"Oh, of course," she said, "the famous magician. Some of the members of my bridge club have been to your performance. They were quite impressed with your tricks."

"They are illusions, Miss Bess. Not tricks. May I ask why you have not graced one of my performances with your presence?"

"Illusions. Forgive me, Mr. Peterfreund. I'm not much of one for such things. I prefer the world anchored in reality."

As ominous as the magician's sudden appearance felt, Nell couldn't help shooting her mother-in-law an amused look. Anchored in reality? Bess Marchand had consulted Joseph Calendar for years to speak through him to her dead husband, and it was she who had insisted that Nell first visit the medium herself. Bess returned her look with one of such innocence that Nell almost laughed.

Any such inclination left her when she realized that Waldo was studying her again.

"Miss Nell, I would also be honored if you would accompany Miss Bess to one of my performances. I can arrange for the best seats in the theatre if you will only tell me when you'd like to attend."

Nell struggled to calm her voice, which threatened to shake. She would not let him know how much he unsettled her. "Thank you, but I'm not much of one for magic acts either."

"A pity. I would so like to share my art with you." A frigid smile played over his lips. "I wish I knew where we've met."

"I don't believe we have. I don't think I could have forgotten you."

Choosing to accept her remark as a compliment, Waldo gave her a courtly bow.

"Have you been in Memphis before, Mr. Peterfreund?" Bess said, still playing the hostess. "Perhaps you and Nell met at a ball or some other social occasion."

"No, Miss Bess. This is my first stay in this Memphis." He pulled a visiting card from an ornate silver case he held in his hand and presented it to Nell. "May I call on you, Mrs. Marchand?"

She kept her hands clasped tightly in her lap. "No, Mr. Peterfreund. I am recently widowed and still in mourning. I do not receive callers at home."

This time it was Bess who gawked at Nell.

"I see," Waldo said. "Of course, I would not dream of intruding on you in your grief. It seems I must admire you from afar."

"Yes, it seems you must. Now, if you will pardon us, Mr. Peterfreund, our ice cream is melting."

"Should you have a change of heart, you can reach me at the Peabody." Placing the card on the table, the magician bowed again, turned, and stalked out the door.

"You weren't very kind to him, Nell," Bess said when he had gone.

Shivering, Nell looked at the dish of ice cream in front of her and pushed it aside.

"The last thing in this world I want is that man in our house, Mother. Or anywhere near me. The Amazing Waldo makes my skin crawl."

CHAPTER 41

With his reaction to the magician at Calpurnia's funeral and his later warnings about him in mind, Nell was reluctant to tell Joseph Calendar of their encounter with Waldo Peterfreund at the Arcade. The alarm on his face when she did persuaded her that she might have done better not to.

At his doorstep, she passed one of the ladies from Bess's bridge club whom she knew from her mother-in-law consulted the medium from time to time. Simon showed Nell to Calendar's lavishly appointed Spirit Room, where he conducted his interviews with clients. She settled herself on the red-tasseled gold-dupioni sofa. He had just offered her a sip of the brandy he kept on hand for those overcome by their communion with their loved ones. Now, the decanter descended with a thunk, and he rushed to stand over her.

"Nell, should he confront you again, please promise me that you will get as far away from him as quickly as you can and will call me at once. He didn't threaten you in any way, did he?"

"Good Lord, Joseph, now you're scaring me. I told Mother I can't stand the sight of him, but I didn't think we were in any actual danger."

Calendar hesitated, obviously contemplating how best to respond. "Nell, remember I've told you he can be ruthless. It's simple prudence not to want you to have anything to do with Waldo."

"Believe me, having anything to do with him is the last thing I'm thinking about."

"Good. If he approaches you again–"

"Yes, I know. Call you immediately." She studied him. "Joseph, is there something about this man that you're not telling me? You said you knew him from before. If he's truly dangerous, shouldn't I know so I can prepare myself?"

Calendar sighed, rubbed a hand across his eyes, and suddenly looked so tired that Nell had to fight the urge to stand, cup his face in her hands, and tell him that everything would be all right.

"Nell," he said, "my past with Waldo is too painful to recount in detail. Will you respect that?"

"Of course, Joseph. Forgive me. I didn't mean to pry."

She drew back and folded her hands in her lap.

"Nell–" He sat beside her.

"It's all right, Joseph. Really. I don't want to overstep our friendship."

He searched her face, looking for what, she couldn't say. Keeping her eyes on his, she waited.

At last, he spoke, his voice detached, almost cold. "You've heard me mention a gifted young medium I worked with in Vienna."

"Yes."

"Her name was Sarah. Waldo caused her to take her own life."

"Oh, Joseph. I'm so sorry. Was she . . . was she more than your teacher?"

"I was never her student, Nell. I was Sarah's husband."

His voice was calm, almost detached, but the anguish of the words tore her. She held herself as still as she could, her nails digging into her palms, longing for him to go on but praying that he wouldn't.

"We met at the university," he said. "I was studying Egyptian history. Sarah was a philosophy student, the daughter of an eminent Jewish doctor, a specialist in studies of the brain. Her family didn't approve of me, of course. They had a young industrialist from among her own people in mind for her. But Sarah was strong-willed. Headstrong, her father would have said. She left the comfort and luxury of his house to live with me. They never forgave me for taking her from them.

"We had known each other about a year when she had her first vision. I had some knowledge of such things, and I knew people in spiritualist circles in the city. Together we guided her. Her gift was great, the greatest I had ever encountered until I met you.

"But underneath that show of will there was a sensitivity, a fragility that no one suspected. No one but Waldo, that is. He knew just how to manipulate her insecurities. When I realized what was happening, it was too late. Waldo had persuaded her that what she thought was her gift was madness. He helped her father take her from my home and put her into treatment with Sigmund Freud. You may have heard of him."

"He has something to do with the mind."

"Precisely. Freud developed a method of talking with his patients to help them change their behavior and overcome their difficulties. He is brilliant, of course, but there was no room in his world for the kind of gift that Sarah had. He tried to cure her. You know as well as anyone that the gift cannot be denied, but she did her best to. When she could not still the voices in her head or the visions, she flung herself from the top of St. Stephen's Cathedral."

Nell squeezed her eyes shut against the pain in his, against the image of his Sarah lying broken and bleeding on the cobblestones.

"So, you see, Nell, just how ruthless Waldo can be," he said, urgency creeping into his voice. "Perhaps now you understand why I want to keep you safe from him. I failed Sarah. I could not bear it if I failed you as well."

"Joseph, oh my Lord, you didn't fail her. If Sarah was ill, what happened to her could have happened no matter what you did. Even if you had never met. Waldo was simply the catalyst. You have to forgive yourself."

"I have tried, Nell. Perhaps with time, I can."

She knew so little about him, really, but she had some idea of what it had cost him to tell her about his wife. They had both suffered in this life. But Joseph had loved and had that love torn from him. Her heart ached for him in a way it had not when Ellis died. Their love had never been real, but she had lost her illusion of Ellis. When he was gone, she had been relieved, felt emancipated. Perhaps that had been wrong of her.

Nell let her fingers come to rest on his forearm. "I am truly sorry." He glanced down at her hand on his arm, smiled at her.

"Thank you. But that is the past. You and I are very much in the present, and I am determined to do everything I can to keep you safe from Waldo."

"What can he do to me? Try to drive me mad, too? I'm not afraid of the Amazing Waldo."

"Believe me, if you were, it would be much, much wiser."

CHAPTER 42

They had hardly shut off the lights in the Tabernacle after the Friday night healing service before Mordecai Jones had heard from at least half a dozen people that Henry Barcroft had inherited Sister Louise's gift from the Lord. Helping Mordecai prepare Saturday afternoon for his first sermon at the Tabernacle of Light on Sunday morning, Evelina was abuzz with it.

"You know, Brother Jones, I've been working with the Tabernacle almost since the beginning, and it reminded me of the old days when Sister must have cured 10 or 20 people at a time. They used to line up around the block by noon on Friday just to get in the door. Came from all over the country to see her heal folks or to be healed themselves.

"Of course, folks don't put as much stock in faith healing now as they did when Sister was just starting out. Friday night, we didn't have more than, say, 50 or 60 people in the congregation, but I bet you anything we'll have at least twice that many for the service this Friday. You could practically see the power flowing through Henry's hands. There was a glow to his face that reminded me of those old-time stained glass windows with the halos around Jesus and the apostles. It was something to see."

Evelina fussed around Mordecai for a while, adjusting the height of the microphone and checking the view of him in the pulpit from the back row of the sanctuary.

"You're taller even than Sister, and that's saying something. She's the tallest woman I ever did see, taller than my daddy by a good 2

165

inches at least. Did you know that she has to have her shoes special made? Tall woman like her has big feet. Before we were getting enough contributions to give us a little breathing room, I heard tell she used to go down to Lowenstein's and buy men's shoes because they were the only ones that fit her. I think that's one reason she got to favoring the floor-length robes, too, so people couldn't see she what she had on her feet.

"Of course, now she goes to the Italian shoemaker over in Germantown that does a lot of shoes for the society ladies. Not that she's extravagant. But standing up the way she does all during the service, she's got to have something comfortable. That Italian knows just how to fashion a heel right so it looks pretty but doesn't hurt her.

"Now for me, it doesn't matter what I wear on my feet. Nobody's going to be looking at my shoes, at least not here at the Tabernacle. Last Christmas, though, Sister needed something special. We were going to fly her across the stage as part of the pageant. She was going to play one of the Heavenly Host welcoming the Christ Child, and she knew people in the congregation would be able to see her feet when she passed overhead. She told Luigi—that's the shoemaker's name, Luigi— that she needed some kind of slipper that looked like an angel would wear it. He made her these little silver shoes that looked just like that, and he was so proud of them. He told her he fixed them up special so she could wear them to a party, too, if she wanted to get more than just one use out of them. Sister is practical like that. Everything she uses in the services is something that can be worn again or go to charity.

"Anyway, Luigi took one look at my work boots—I was still in my coveralls—and told me that wasn't anything a nice lady like me should have on her feet. He made me a pair of slippers just like the ones Sister Louise wore in the pageant. That's what I wear now if I go out somewhere special."

The whole time she chattered, Evelina adjusted the special microphone overhead so everyone could hear Mordecai if he decided to get down from the pulpit and wander across the stage the way Sister

Louise liked to do sometimes. She had him stand on the block that she had made for Sister so she looked even taller from the pulpit than she already was. She decided Mordecai didn't need it.

"We have you standing on that, and you're going to look like a stork."

When she had everything adjusted the way she wanted it, the stage manager told him she was going up to the back row of the balcony to be sure she could hear him even if he whispered. "All right, now, when I get up there, I'm going to wave at you, and that will be your signal to start your sermon. I want you to talk the way you're going to talk in the morning. Don't holler or anything. Let the microphones do the work for you."

She scampered away, and Mordecai squinted against the lights, watching for her to signal to him. When she was in place, she waved.

He cleared his throat a time or two to be sure his voice was going to come out right. "Brothers and sisters," he said, "my name is Brother Mordecai Jones, and I welcome you to the Tabernacle of Light. If the Lord blesses us as I pray He will here today, then the work we do together will be mighty indeed."

"That's perfect," Evelina hollered down from the balcony. "I could hear every word. You know, you've got a nice speaking voice. There's a very pleasing masculine tone to it. Hang on, and I'll come down and unhook you. Now that we've got everything just right, I want to leave the microphones positioned the way they are so we don't have too much setting up to do in the morning."

Mordecai looked out over the empty sanctuary, imagining what it would be like the next morning, filled with people waiting to hear him bring them the Word. The Tabernacle would hold almost 6,000, and he knew there had been a time when it was filled every Sunday. Now, he would be sure that there was never an empty seat again. This was the spotlight he was meant for. He'd known it from the day Sister Louise had come to Tiptonville, and he had felt her speaking just to him.

This was where he had always belonged. *Thank you, Lord, for bringing me here. Look down on me and guide me to do Your will. Help me to spread the word of Your love.*

The stage manager was back at his side, giving the microphone one last tweak and carrying the block off the stage to store it until Sister Louise needed it again.

"All right, Brother Jones, Sister asked me to look after you. The night before a big sermon, she likes to go eat a nice steak. Says it gives her the strength for the day's work to come. I think tomorrow's going to be an important day for you and for the Tabernacle. I think I should be sure you get fed proper. How about that?"

Mordecai had never been anywhere fancier to eat than country restaurants that served meat and three. Now he was sitting at a booth in Jim's Place with Evelina across the table from him. The waitress set a platter in front of him with the biggest steak on it that he had ever seen.

"Well, go on," Evelina said. "Don't just sit there looking at it. Cut into the thing. You've got the Lord's work to do tomorrow, and you can't do it on an empty stomach."

THE NEXT MORNING, MORDECAI DRESSED IN THE WHITE ROBE WITH the red cross that was the emblem of the Tabernacle of Light. He hadn't asked for a black robe right off because he wanted to establish himself first. There would be time enough to change how they did things at the Tabernacle. Waiting offstage for his cue to go on, the preacher tried to judge the size of the crowd by the echo of the hall. Evelina adjusted his stole, which had slipped a little off to one side. He wasn't used to wearing robes. His plain black suit had always been good enough.

"We've got a pretty good crowd out there today," she said. "They must have heard you would be preaching and came down to see what you can do. Don't be nervous. Sister wouldn't have asked you to come to the Tabernacle if she didn't have faith that the Lord had sent you to carry on her work."

"His work."

"That's what I meant. All right now. Here you go. And remember that you don't need to holler. Let the microphone carry your voice for you. Holler too loud, and you'll split people's eardrums."

She gave him a little push, and Mordecai started up the steps to the pulpit. Looking out over the sanctuary, he saw what looked like a sea of faces, all turned toward him. The lights took a little getting used to, but he could make out a few members of his congregation scattered among the faithful of the Tabernacle. Grasping the edges of the pulpit, he smiled out at the crowd. "Brothers and sisters," he said, "my name is Mordecai Jones, and I welcome you to the Tabernacle of Light."

CHAPTER 43

Sometimes as the accuser, sometimes as the accused, Waldo had dealt with the law all over the world. As police stations went, the headquarters of the Memphis Police was almost pleasant. It was clean, windows let in plenty of light, and the officers were well dressed. Sergeant Arnold Acker in particular exuded an air of decency and authority. In contrast to that long, sad face of his, he also had a certain sartorial style that spoke of a woman's touch, a woman with taste. Waldo suspected that the sergeant had married above himself. Good for you, Sergeant Acker, he thought.

Officer Murphy interrupted his reverie.

"All right then, Mr. Peterfreund," the officer said, "Let's go over this again. Begin at the beginning."

"After all the time we've spent together, Officer Murphy, don't you think it's time we called each other by our first names? Mine is Waldo. Or the Amazing Waldo, if you prefer. What's yours?"

That elicited a smile at least. "All right, Waldo. Mine's Eugene."

"Would you believe me, Eugene, if I told you again that I am innocent?" Waldo said. "It would save us all a lot of time."

"They all say they're innocent," Murphy said. "Everybody we get in here is innocent. Amazing how that works, isn't it?"

"But, look, what advantage would there be for me in killing those people?"

"Maybe you like doing it for fun."

"Wouldn't it be rather obvious given that each of them had made an

170

appearance at one of my performances and then outside my theatre?"

"Maybe you're one of those fellas that wants to get caught. Maybe you're just daring us to do it."

"I think that would put a rather unpleasant end to my stage career. A career I've worked too long to nurture and develop. Come now, Eugene. That can't really make sense to you."

"Who said crime makes any sense?" Acker said, stepping in to break up what was rapidly degenerating into a comedy routine. "You want to know what I think, Waldo?"

"I hang upon your every word, Arnold."

"I think you enjoy luring people you see as weak to your shows. You butter them up, make them feel like they're doing something special by getting them up on stage with you, and then you knock them off. It's how you get your jollies.

"That is a fascinating theory, but how do you explain the fact that I have performed my act for more than 10 years without so much as a peep of trouble, let alone any suggestion of murder? If I went around the country knocking off, as you say, the unfortunates among us, don't you think someone would have noticed by now? The problem is, you and Eugene here have focused on the wrong man. Once you've made up your minds, it seems no power on earth, no incontrovertible proof, can change them. Why, I imagine that the real killer could come in here with whom? Let's say a blind girl. We haven't had one of those yet. Let's say he comes in with a blind girl, seats her on your captain's desk in full view of the entire squad room, and garrotes her while she screams her head off. Or at least screams for a bit before he cuts off her air supply. I don't think even that would be enough to persuade you that I'm innocent."

"If you had an alibi, it might be different," Officer Murphy said.

"Oh, but I do."

"What? You never said anything about that."

"Well, if you think carefully about it, Eugene, you and our good Sergeant Acker here have never actually asked me what I was doing each time one of the victims was killed. You were so busy asking me if I murdered them, climbing all over and under my stage, and making up your mind that I had that you've never asked me where I was. Not once."

By this time, poor Eugene had blushed a tomato hue that might have been attractive on a slimmer man but made him look like nothing so much as a fire hydrant. Arnold Acker pushed his fedora back so far—a habit Waldo had noticed he adopted when he thought deeply about something—that it actually fell off the back of his head. The sergeant picked up Murphy's notebook, the one the officer wrote in so carefully and diligently almost without ceasing, and flipped through the pages.

"Well, I'll be dadgum," Acker said. "He's right. That changes everything, you know. If you've actually got alibis for the times of all the murders, Mr. Peterfreund—"

"Waldo."

"If you've got an alibi for each one, Waldo, then we'd have no choice but to believe you. Unless, of course, you claimed the same alibi for each one."

"Ah, then, we're in luck. I do have the same alibi for each murder, Arnold, but fortunately for me, it was with a different young woman every time, if you understand my meaning. You see, after my long-time assistant Matilda abandoned me, I was forced to, shall we say, interview a series of young women for the job. There are certain abilities that I find mandatory in an assistant, and I had to be absolutely sure that I had the right girl."

"Son of a–," Murphy said.

"Now, Eugene, there's no reason to resort to profanity. I can give you their names, of course. The only thing I ask is that you keep this little detail out of the papers. I'd hate to see some pretty young girl's reputation ruined when, really, it's such a little thing when you come down to it. Americans are so puritanical, you know. There are some cultures that value experience in a woman. Some, in fact, in which a man refuses to marry until a woman has borne him at least one child as proof of her fertility. When you consider it from a logical standpoint, it's really quite sensible."

"All right, Waldo," Officer Murphy said. "What are their names?"

"Did you want all of them, or just the ones I was with at the times of the murders?"

"Let's keep it simple," Sergeant Acker said. "Just give us the names that correspond with the murders. I can assign only so many men to this case, you know."

Waldo threw back his head and laughed out loud. "Oh, Arnold, you delight me. How wonderful that you have a sense of humor and can maintain it even in the face of what must feel like failure."

"I'm glad you're amused."

"Oh, I am, indeed. Eugene, are you ready?"

"Shoot," Murphy said.

Afterward, Waldo did feel a little bad about having to divulge the names of the young women he'd been with. Ordinarily, he wasn't the type to kiss and tell. One had one's standards, after all. But these were unusual circumstances, to say the least. He was sure each of them would understand. And if Arnold Acker had promised his discretion, well, Waldo was sure the whole thing would be handled delicately.

"The sarge says you can go while we check these out," Officer Murphy said.

"Thank you, Eugene. I don't know about you, but I have the awfullest time falling asleep for the first night or two in a strange bed. I imagine that jailhouse mattresses do not set the standard of comfort I'm accustomed to. I'm grateful that I'm to be allowed to return to my suite at the Peabody and my bed there. I think I've finally gotten the pillow to just the right degree of softness to ensure a good night's sleep."

With that, the magician rose and strolled from the room as though nothing in the world troubled him. Acker almost admired him.

"You know, Murphy, Waldo talks more than just about anybody I've ever seen. Only about half of it makes sense, but you have to respect a fella that can go on and on like that. It's almost like being hypnotized."

"Yeah, it's like I told you. I ain't never seen anything like it."

"HOW COME YOU THINK WALDO WAITED SO LONG TO TELL US ABOUT his alibis, Acker?" Murphy said, stopping by the sergeant's office on his way out to catch the trolley home.

"He was playing with us. I think he wanted to see just how far down the path he could lead us."

"You think he would have let us get all the way to charging him?"

"Maybe, but I think he would have stopped us before we got to the point of a trial. The man likes to be in the limelight, no doubt about it, but once he was at trial, who knows? Maybe he couldn't count on those girls to back up his story once we had him up for murder."

Acker flipped the notebook closed and returned it to Murphy, who slipped it into his shirt pocket.

"You know, I'm glad his alibis all checked out. Talking to him was just about to wear me clean jab out. And he's one less suspect to worry about."

"Since you're so relieved, why don't you get back to figuring out who really killed those folks?"

"Yes, sir." Murphy touched two fingers to his brow and turned to go. "I'll get right on that, Sarge."

Alone in his office, Arnold Acker couldn't shake the feeling that there was still something not right about Waldo Peterfreund. Something he'd better keep an eye on if he knew what was good for him.

CHAPTER 44

When a call came for Nell from Arnold Acker, Calendar was with her in her sitting room.

"It seems we're out of suspects," Nell said, returning from the front hall. "Sergeant Acker has cleared Waldo, so you were right about him. And Louise Henslowe has gone to Florida for a rest cure."

"Unless she left for fear of being caught," Calendar said.

"Still can't believe she had anything to do with the killings."

"Ambition can be a powerful motivation, and the need to punish those who thwart it, even more so. If Sister Louise's influence had been waning as drastically as you believe it has, Nell, she could be desperate."

"Then why didn't she just kill Waldo? Especially after that stunt with pretending to restore McCrory's leg, which he so clearly staged to humiliate her."

"He is too public a figure now to spirit away easily, and he provides an effective foil for her sermons against the evils of magic. Killing those who have dealt with him could be meant as a warning to those contemplating doing the same."

"Well, that sure hasn't worked. People are still flocking to see the Amazing Waldo's act down at the Odeon." Nell plopped down on the sofa, rubbing her temples. "Oh, this is all giving me a headache. Besides, I'm almost positive the figure with Calpurnia in my vision was a man."

"Then, perhaps we should consider the two contenders for the Tabernacle of Light that Sister Louise left behind, Mordecai Jones and Henry Barcroft. Jones's association with Waldo seems evidence of his ambition, but we can assume that either would want to inherit a healthy church when he dons her white robe."

"Robes!" Nell said, sitting up. "That's what I saw. The man who took Calpurnia away must have been wearing a minister's robe. Oh, Joseph, I think you're right. It could be someone from the Tabernacle. It just didn't occur to me because I'm so accustomed to our pastor wearing black. But Sister Louise has always worn those white robes with the red crosses on the front. It's her trademark."

She flopped back against the sofa. "But everyone in the Tabernacle of Light choir wears white robes, and so do all the ushers and the stagehands. It could have been any one of them. Lordy mercy, we were better off when we thought it was the Amazing Waldo or Sister Louise. Now we're not out of suspects, we have dozens."

CHAPTER 45

That Friday evening, the crowds at the Tabernacle of Light might not have rivaled those of its glory days, but the numbers in the sanctuary were 10 times what they had been the week before. For Henry Barcroft, it was confirmation that he had been chosen to carry on the Lord's work.

At the altar, he now stood, arms outstretched. "Who among you wishes to be healed? Come forward."

A middle-aged woman in a faded yellow gingham dress stepped into the aisle from a pew near the front of the congregation, pulling along a boy in a blue-and-white striped work shirt who looked to be about 16. The boy held his right arm against his chest, the hand twisted into a claw. His head tilted down and left so that he had to turn his eyes up and to the right to see where he was going. As they approached, he worked his lower jaw back and forth, moaning. Watching them make their way onto the stage, the preacher sent up a silent prayer that Jesus would be on his side that night.

"Is this your son?" Henry said, touching the woman's elbow when they had joined him.

"Yessir. This is my boy Wendell. Wendell Pettitt."

At the sound of his name, the boy shuffled closer to his mother, who reached up to stroke his hair.

Something familiar about the woman stopped Henry, and he peered closely at her. "Have we met before, sister? Are you a regular worshipper here at the Tabernacle with us?"

"No, sir, Reverend." The woman shifted her feet, glancing out at the congregation before she met his eyes. "We heard tell of some of the healing you had done and came all the way from DeWitt over in Arkansas this morning, hoping you could help Wendell. Can you heal him?"

Henry held her gaze for a long moment, struggling to think where he must have seen her. She returned a look of such careworn innocence that he decided he must have been mistaken.

"It's the Lord who will heal him, sister. Not I. What is your name?"

"Virgie Pettit."

"What afflicts your Wendell, Miss Virgie?"

She put her arm around the boy's shoulders. "When he was 10, his daddy got him up on the barn roof to help him nail down a piece of tin that blew off in a storm. Wendell got to playing around up there like a boy will and fell off right onto his head. Didn't stir an inch for two whole days, and his daddy and I thought sure he was going to die. Been like this ever since he woke up. Course, his daddy never should have had him up there in the first place and blames himself something awful for what happened. Doctor back home said there was nothing he could do for Wendell. It's been mighty hard on us, him being our only boy 'n all."

A murmur swelled up from the congregation, and Henry felt his own heart squeeze in sympathy.

"Do you trust in the Lord?"

"Yes, Reverend."

Henry reached out to put his hands on the boy's head, but Wendell grunted and tried to back away.

"It's all right, baby," Virgie said, patting him. "Hold still. Reverend Henry wants to help you."

The boy did as he was told.

Henry grasped each of his shoulders. "Lord, look down on this poor boy, take pity on him, and make him whole."

At first, nothing happened. Henry felt only the rough cloth of Wendell's work shirt under his hands. Then, the boy began to stir, to shake. He pulled away from Henry to step toward the edge of the stage. Wendell's head came up, and he looked out at the congregation, eyes widening. His arm straightened. His hand untwisted. He wiggled his fingers, looking at them as though they must belong to someone else.

"Hallelujah!" someone at the back of the sanctuary called out.

Virgie's hands went up to her face. "Wendell?"

"Mama?" he said, turning back toward her.

"Praise Jesus! It's a puredee old miracle!" She grabbed Henry's hand and pumped it. "Bless you, Reverend." Then she pulled Wendell into her arms, weeping loudly. "Oh, my baby!"

Cries of "Hallelujah" and "Praise the Lord" echoed through the sanctuary.

Only Henry stood still, his arms hanging limp at his sides. He had seen Virgie before, and he had worked out exactly where.

CHAPTER 46

Henry Barcroft turned and bolted from the stage. Virgie and Wendell stood looking after him, then faced each other, undecided what to do next. When the preacher made no sign of returning, the stage manager stepped out and spoke quietly with them. She motioned for one of the stagehands, who led them off out of sight.

It took Evelina several moments to calm the congregation, which began to stamp their feet and call for Henry's return.

"Now, folks, I don't think there's anything to worry about. Brother Henry was probably just so overcome with joy at Jesus's healing that poor boy that he needed some time alone with the Lord. Y'all go on home now, and be sure to tell all your friends about the miracle you witnessed here tonight."

She waited until the last worshipper had shuffled out and she had sent the choir and all the stagehands home before she went looking for him. She found him sitting at Sister Louise's desk, looking as though the Last Trump had just sounded and Jesus had not called him home to heaven to sit at his right hand among the elect.

"What happened out there?"

"That woman you sent up and her son, they were frauds." Henry's voice shook.

"What are you talking about?"

"Not two weeks ago, they came here, looking for a handout, and we fed them. Sister asked you to find them a place to stay."

"Those aren't the same folks, Henry–"

He leapt up and slammed his fist down on the desk so hard that Evelina took two steps back.

"Don't lie to me!" he said, his face going crimson. "You paid those people to come up to the altar tonight and pretend that the boy needed healing."

The stage manager put up her hands to placate him. "Now, Henry, there's nothing to be upset about. I just thought that you might need a little help believing in yourself. If you do, then it's easier for the people in the congregation to believe in you, too."

"Did you do that for Sister Louise as well?"

"Only a few times, when we first came back to Memphis. You know how down in the dumps she was after we had to close the other Tabernacles. She just needed something to get her going again."

"So, she is a fake?" Henry made a sound somewhere between a sob and a gurgle, sat down hard on the chair, and buried his face in his hands.

"She cured some of them," Evelina said. "And she had cured hundreds before that. I just greased the wheels to keep the faithful coming back . . . and to keep Louise believing in herself."

"Are you telling me she never knew what you were doing?"

"Well, we never talked about it in front of her, but she's a smart woman. Long as it's been going on, she might have noticed something. It doesn't change anything that we've done here."

"But all these years, you've been cheating people. Making them believe something that wasn't true."

"Who's to say so, son? You've believed in Sister Louise all this time, and you helped that mute girl. Maybe believing really was all folk needed to let the Lord work in them."

"And what about that girl I healed last week?" He wiped his face on his sleeve and stared down at his hands. "Was she one of your shills?"

"No, Henry. I had nothing to do with her. If she really couldn't talk, then something you did gave her back her speech. That's why all those people came to see you tonight. They were hoping for another miracle."

"Why couldn't you leave us alone?" His face contorted, Henry stood and started toward Evelina. "Get out!"

She turned and ran.

CHAPTER 47

As fond as he was growing of Nell Marchand, it took Arnold Acker all the self-control he could muster to stifle the groan that threatened to escape him at the sight of her standing in his doorway again, Joseph Calendar at her side.

"Miss Nell, what can I do for you folks?"

"Sergeant, I think we may have an idea who killed Calpurnia and the others. Or at least an idea of where to find him."

"Where is that, Miss Nell?"

"At the Tabernacle of Light."

Acker reached for his notebook and pencil. "All right. Why don't you come on in and tell me about it?"

By the time she wound down, he decided there might be something to this Tabernacle of Light business. "It'll take us some time to work through all the people there, but if we start with Jones and Barcroft, we just might shake something loose. I'll talk to my captain and see if he can't let me have a couple more men to help with interviews if we need them." He consulted his watch. "It's getting on to too late in the day now, but I'll see which of the fellas might be interested in Saturday duty. We'll get on it first thing tomorrow."

Nell Marchand and Joseph Calendar exchanged a look, and Acker would bet money that there was more to her story than she was letting on.

CHAPTER 48

In his office at the Tabernacle of Light, Henry Barcroft unlocked his desk and took out the bottle of special whiskey he kept hidden there. From one of the drawers, he extracted a flask and filled it.

His canvas satchel was on the top shelf of the closet. He took it down and unfastened the leather straps to check its contents. Satisfied that he had everything he needed, he pocketed the flask, pushed the satchel out of sight under the desk, and went in search of Evelina. Saturday choir practice was over, and the last of the stagehands had gone home to their families, but she would still be working in the sanctuary, checking one last time to be sure she had everything just right for the Sunday morning service. He was going to pay her a visit, tell her he wanted to let bygones be bygones, and offer her a drink to say thank you for all her loyal service to Sister Louise through the years. He knew she took a secret tipple now and then, so he had no doubt that she would be willing to toast to peace between them. Sister might be a steadfast supporter of temperance, but Sister wasn't here to protest.

None of it had been real. Sister Louise had never healed him, might not ever have healed anyone. It didn't matter if she believed she had. It was all ruined.

And now the police had come with more questions about the fake cripple and the others, asking to talk to everyone who worked with the church. It should never have come to this—would never have—if he had known the Tabernacle of Light was built on a foundation of lies.

CHAPTER 49

The sound of Bess Marchand coughing carried down the hall of the Marchand house to the back sitting room where Nell read in companionable silence with Joseph Calendar, she with her Agatha Christie and he with a book on the history of the Ottoman Empire. In search of relief from the darkness that had hung over the household since Calpurnia's death, the three planned an outing to see "King Kong," which was back for a return engagement at the Warner Theater on Main Street.

"Lord have mercy," Nell said, setting aside *The Murder at the Vicarage.* "I believe Mother would cough her lungs straight up out of her mouth and across the room before she'd take anything to make her feel better. I'm going to tell her we're having an afternoon sherry and ask if she wants to join us. Maybe that will help. Thank goodness she never joined the WCTU, but, then, the Judge did enjoy his whiskey."

"I'll do the honors," Calendar said. He fetched a third glass from the cabinet, unstopped the sherry decanter, and poured the dark liquid.

Nell found Bess in her sewing room, studying the pattern for a new apron for Hattie.

"You know, my dear, those white aprons of hers show every spot of sauce and every pop of grease so badly. I think something in a cheerful blue check or gingham would be lovely and so much more practical, don't you?"

"If you can get her to wear them. You know Hattie has her own ideas about how she should dress to serve company. Nothing but starched white pinafores and those caps that make her look like a nurse will do."

"Yes, Nell, but these could be her everyday aprons. I could–" Bess broke off in a fit of coughing.

"Mother, why don't you rest a bit with us before we go to the pictures? Joseph and I are having a glass of sherry. Wouldn't you like some, too?"

"You know, that does sound good." Bess dabbed at her lips with her handkerchief. "I am a little tired, and I do enjoy cream sherry."

"I know you do." Nell took her mother-in-law's hands, pulled her up from her chair, and put an arm around her shoulders.

Bess settled in a chair by the sitting room window, sipping the sherry Calendar had served her. The medium brought the decanter to Nell. "May I refresh yours?"

"Just a tiny drop, please."

Calendar took her glass, poured the requested drop, and returned it.

Nell's hand closed around the stem, and the sitting room vanished.

Under the stage, the air smelled of sawdust and new-sawn wood. Moving as quickly as he dared, he pulled the woman along. He could not risk her falling and crying out. At last they were clear, and she could stand upright. She braced herself with her cane. Behind them, the magician's voice droned on, spouting its drivel about magic and immortality. There was only one road to eternal life.

"Where are we going?" the woman said.

"Not far." He reached into his satchel for the burlap bag, swinging it over her head before she could dodge.

"What–"

He clapped a hand over her mouth and pressed his own against her ear.

"If you fight me or make a sound, I will snap your neck right here. Do you understand?"

She nodded.

He lowered the bag over the rest of her body, pushed her onto her back, and tied it at her feet. No one would know he wasn't just another hand transporting the Amazing Waldo's gear. He picked her up, shrugged her securely over his shoulder, and carried her out into the afternoon light.

In the place he had prepared for her, he sat her in the chair.

"When I remove the bag, you must be perfectly still. I'm going to give you a drink to calm your nerves, and then we'll have a little talk. All right?"

"Yes."

"Good."

He pulled the bag back over her head. She blinked in the light and looked up at him, her eyes enormous in her face.

A face that was not Calpurnia's.

In the sitting room, Nell first noticed the dampness spreading from her right knee down her leg. Her sherry. She must have spilled her sherry.

"Nell?" Calendar's voice was sharp.

"Joseph," she said when she could get her breath again, "we've got to get to the Tabernacle of Light. He's got someone else, and we've got to get there before it's too late." She tried to rise, but again her legs wouldn't hold her.

"Take a moment to recover."

"No, we've got to go now!"

Without another word, he slid his hands behind her back and under her knees, lifting her in his arms and starting toward the door in one motion. The fabric of his jacket was rough under her cheek. *Tweed.*

"Miss Bess, call the police station and tell them someone is in danger at the Tabernacle of Light and that we're on our way there." Careful not to bump Nell's knees, he passed through the doorway and raced toward the front hall. "Jenkins!"

The driver burst from the kitchen, a silver knife and a polishing cloth in his hands. "Yes, sir?"

"The car, now!"

Jenkins disappeared through the kitchen door, not stopping to answer.

"Joseph–"

"We'll be there in time, Nell. Put your arms around my neck."

She did as he said. He released her back long enough to open the front door and push through just as Jenkins roared up to the foot of the steps in the Duesenberg and slammed to a stop.

CHAPTER 50

Evelina Milam pulled at the restraints that bound her to the chair in Henry's office. *Please, Lord, forgive me for my sins and deliver me from this poor, sick boy.*

"I tie a good knot, Evelina." He watched her across the desk, his face solemn and his eyes desolate.

"You sure do." She tried to laugh, but it came out sounding more like a wheeze. "Look, Henry, everything I did was for Sister Louise and the Tabernacle so we could all serve the Lord."

"The Lord hates a liar. My father always said so. Liars deserve whatever happens to them."

Her mouth went as dry as week-old bread. She licked her lips, trying to think. "After everything she's done for you, Henry, you don't want to hurt Sister and the Tabernacle. What I did was wrong, I see that now, but if you kill me, you'll destroy everything she worked so hard to build. That you've worked so hard for."

"Are you thirsty, Evelina?" He reached for the whiskey bottle that sat on his desk and poured some into a glass. "Why don't you just have a sip of this?"

"Now, you know I don't drink spirits. Sister doesn't approve of drinking. Couldn't you fetch me a glass of water from the kitchen?" If she could stall him, she might be able to scoot the chair over to the window, break the glass somehow, and scream for help.

A regretful smile, the kind a parent gives a child trying to wiggle out of whatever she's been caught doing, played across his lips. "But I know you do. That's another lie."

She sent up another silent prayer. *Lord, if you save me, I promise I will never touch another drop as long as I live.*

He scooted the glass across the desk toward her. "I will untie your hands if you promise to be a good girl and not try to run. I'd only catch you anyway. You just have your drink while we talk things over."

Maybe he wasn't going to kill her after all. She nodded. "OK, Henry. I know we can figure this out."

Her bonds cut, she rubbed her wrists. He held the whiskey out to her. She reached for it, trying to calm the shaking in her hands.

"Thank you."

"It's all going to be all right, Evelina." He put his hand on her shoulder.

She raised the glass toward her lips, the whiskey smell burning her nose a little the way it always did.

Behind her, she heard the door burst open and slam against the wall. Startled, Henry turned toward the sound. Evelina flung herself to the right and scrambled away from him.

"Stop right there, son," a man's voice said.

"You have no right to be here," Henry said.

"I said stop."

Evelina had never heard a gunshot except at the movies. It sounded like the end of the world. She turned in time to see Henry Barcroft sprawl across the carpet. From under his body oozed a dark pool that she knew had to be blood.

CHAPTER 51

Nell and Calendar were at the station until well into the afternoon, going over the day's events at the Tabernacle of Light.

"Miss Nell, I feel like you ought to be the one wearing the detective's badge. I still don't know how you figured out it was Henry Barcroft who killed those people, let alone how you knew he was about to do the same to that Milam woman. Either you're the smartest woman who ever walked the face of the earth, or you really are psychic."

"Arnold . . . Sergeant Acker, I just had a hunch. Call it woman's intuition if you like."

"Must have been some hunch."

"It was."

"All right, Miss Nell." He knew there had been more to the Evans case than made it into the papers or his case files. This must be the same kind of thing. "I hope one of these days, you'll take me into your confidence. Meanwhile, I'd be right glad if you called me by my first name. Seems about time, after everything we've been through together these last six months."

"Thank you, Arnold. And I hope you will call me Nell."

"I'd like to take Mrs. Marchand home," Calendar said. "She must be exhausted."

"Of course," Acker said, standing. "I can always call if something comes up."

"And you'll let us know what Evelina Milam says, won't you?"

"Soon as they let me talk to her down at the hospital. They gave her something to make her sleep."

Nell took his hands in hers. "Thank you, Arnold. Knowing that we've caught Calpurnia's killer will give Hattie the kind of peace she hasn't had in weeks. It will give us all peace."

He felt a blush start at the base of his neck and begin working its way up. "Yes, ma'am. And once Doc Mills finishes with that bottle of whiskey, I'll let you know if anything was in it beside bourbon."

The sergeant stood in his doorway, watching Joseph Calendar escort Nell Marchand through the duty room and wondered if there were such a thing as the true sight.

CHAPTER 52

Phoning Sister Louise at that fancy hotel in Florida was just about the hardest thing she'd ever had to do, but there was no help for it. Evelina couldn't let her find out what happened with Henry from a story in the newspaper or, worse yet, from some smart alec reporter calling her to get his own. Sister insisted on catching the next train to Memphis.

At Union Station, Evelina waited for her, hoping no one else would spot Sister. But the shrunken creature who stumbled from the train onto the platform and shambled toward her bore so little resemblance to the dignified woman the stage manager had worked with for 20 years that she almost didn't recognize Louise Henslowe herself. Deep lines had carved themselves at the corners of her mouth, and her eyes looked sunken.

"Hello, Evelina."

"Come on, honey. Let's get you home."

"I need to go to the Tabernacle."

"That can wait. Mordecai is doing the service today."

"I need to talk to him."

Evelina took Sister's train case from her. "Then we'll go to the Tabernacle."

THE STAGE MANAGER DID HER BEST TO PREPARE MORDECAI FOR THE changes in Louise, but he was still shocked when he saw how worn out she looked leaned back in the chair behind her desk, her eyes closed.

"Sister Louise, Evelina said I should come on up after the service."

She opened her eyes. "Do you remember the first time you came to my office, Mordecai? You said you were the answer to my prayers. I didn't know then just how true that was. Now I need your help."

"What can I do for you, Sister?"

"It's time for me to retire. I would like you to take over the Tabernacle, keep it going. Are you willing to do that?"

Mordecai swallowed. "Yes, ma'am." Everything he'd ever dreamed of was going to be his. He felt bad for Sister Louise, real bad, but he would make the Tabernacle of Light the biggest church in Memphis.

"Thank you," she said. "Now, would you mind fetching Evelina, please, Brother? I'm finally ready to go home."

CHAPTER 53

It took a week for everyone at the Marchand house to settle down after what happened with Henry Barcroft at the Tabernacle of Light. Turned out he had poisoned Calpurnia and the others with big doses of codeine masked by the whiskey. Whatever his reasons, they had gone to the grave with him, but Arnold Acker, Nell, and Joseph Calendar figured he'd killed them all out of loyalty to Louise Henslowe. Leaving their bodies behind the Odeon had to have been either an effort to pin the murders on Waldo Peterfreund or to warn him to stay out of Sister Louise's business. With Henry dead, Hattie was almost back to her old self.

In the Marchand kitchen where they sat over the last swallow of their iced tea and planned the evening's menu, Nell told the cook that Joseph Calendar would dine with them, a sort of family commemoration of having brought Calpurnia's killer to justice. Hattie had a soft spot for the medium, and it always tickled her to concoct elaborate meals for him. Tonight of all nights, she said she wanted to fix something extra special. She wanted to prepare squab in fig sauce.

"I canned a bunch of figs for us to eat on this winter, so we've got those. Course, I don't know where on earth we're going to find us any squabs. Seesel's doesn't have them, and if they don't, no other store in Memphis does. I don't know of anybody who raises eating pigeons, do you, Nell?"

"No, I don't think I do. Daddy had a dovecote at the house, but the people who live there now turned it into a potting shed. If we could

195

make do with doves, I might be able to lay hands on some. I could call around, see who's been hunting this weekend."

Hattie frowned. "If I'm going to have to use doves, then I'd better look for a dove recipe. Plenty of pigeons roost down at the Peabody, but I'm not sure I'd want to eat any of them even if they'd let us catch them or go shoot them off the ledges."

"The Peabody!" Nell said. "Of course. Why don't I call down there and see if the chef has squab on the menu?"

"Now, you know I want to fix supper for Dr. Calendar myself. Besides, they're not about to let me into the dining room with y'all."

"I don't mean that we'd go down there to eat. This is your celebration. I bet if I sweet talk the chef, though, he'll let me come get some for our supper. Or at least tell me where to find them."

"That's a good idea." Hattie turned the pages of the cookbook until she came to the section on soups. "On your way back, stop at Piggly Wiggly, please, and pick up a couple of cans of asparagus. This time of year, there isn't going to be any fresh, and I think I'll make asparagus soup for the first course."

A call to the restaurant and a brief chat with the chef secured Hattie's squabs. Jenkins and Nell drove off in quest of the birds.

Behind them, a black Ford sedan pulled away from the curb and slithered into their wake in the traffic headed down Poplar.

CHAPTER 54

At the Peabody, Nell decided to take the back stairs down to the kitchen. If she cut through the lobby to the elevators, she was bound to run into half a dozen people she knew. Jenkins was out front with the Duesenberg running, and she wanted to be quick as she could. She would just run down, thank the chef for the squab, and slip back out before anybody saw her. Then they could swing by Piggly Wiggly and be home in two shakes.

On the landing, Nell stopped to peer into her purse. She'd left in such a hurry that she hadn't thought to check to be sure she had enough money for the birds and everything Hattie wanted from the market. Good. She had a twenty-dollar bill and some ones. That should be more than enough. She snapped the bag closed and started down the next flight.

A hand closed on her right shoulder. She was about to turn to see whose it was when another came across her face from the left and pressed some kind of rag across her nose and mouth. She drew in a breath to scream and tried to claw the rag away from her mouth. Something was wrong with her eyes. Before she could decide what it was, blackness descended.

CHAPTER 55

An hour after they had left for downtown, Jenkins hurried into the kitchen looking worried, an expression Hattie had never seen on his face before.

"Is Miss Nell here?"

"Here?" Hattie said. "Didn't you carry her down to the Peabody to pick up those squabs?"

"I did. She asked me to wait for her out front, said she wouldn't be 15 minutes. When she hadn't come out in 45, I left the car and went down to the kitchens myself to see if she needed any help. Talked to that chef, but he showed me those birds he was holding for her still in their icebox. Said Miss Nell hadn't come in to get them yet. I searched around the hotel lobby and some of the shops, thinking maybe she stopped there even though it wasn't like her not to run in and straight back out again just like she said she was going to do. I asked at the front desk, too. When I couldn't find her, I came right back to the house."

The bottom dropped straight out of Hattie's stomach, and she put down the knife she'd been using to peel the apples for the tarte tatin. "Lord have mercy. What on earth could have happened to that child?"

"I'm right worried, Hattie," the driver said. "I think we should talk to the police."

"All right, but let me call Dr. Calendar first. And don't say anything to Miss Bess yet. I don't want to have to deal with her going to pieces and being hysterical all over the place. I bet Miss Nell is fine, but she would have told you where she was going."

Hattie had a sinking feeling that the Amazing Waldo had something to do with whatever had happened to Nell, but she didn't want to say that to Jenkins because she didn't want to worry him any more than he already was. Not until she had talked to Dr. Calendar.

This time Simon did spray the gravel in the front drive of the Marchand mansion in his haste. The car had not yet come to a complete stop when Calendar was out of the back seat and taking the front stairs three at a time.

He, Jenkins, Simon, and Hattie gathered in the kitchen to go over their plan of action.

"Jenkins, you go to the police," Calendar said. "Tell them everything you've just told us. Simon and I will go to the Peabody and circle out from there around downtown."

"What do you want me to do?" Hattie said.

"I need you to stay here to answer the telephone. It's the only way we'll all be able to communicate with each other. You'll be our command central. And if Miss Bess starts asking questions, you'll need to take care of her. Besides, if Nell comes home, I need you to let her know that we're looking for her."

"Yes, sir, Dr. Calendar."

Calendar knew that Hattie wanted to be out doing something active, searching for Nell, but she understood what had to be done. He also knew that she had the right idea about who had taken her and was itching to go after Waldo herself. He didn't want the added distraction of looking after Hattie when he killed him.

CHAPTER 56

The Odeon Theatre was the oldest in Memphis, having been built by Gustav Meyerlink, one of the first merchant princes to make his fortune in the Bluff City selling dry goods to the riverboat passengers and crews who plied the waters of the mighty Mississippi. A devoted fan of the opera in his native Berlin, he dreamed of raising an opera house on the banks of the great river to rival those of Europe. To it, he would bring the finest voices from around the world. He would commission new works by the most gifted composers. He would make Memphis a cultural mecca.

Tragically for Meyerlink, he died of yellow fever before the first performance could be mounted in his newly finished theatre. His widow, a former chorus member from the Staatsoper Unter den Linden—the Berlin State Opera—decamped to New York, taking her sons and her patronage with her.

Understanding Meyerlink's dream if not quite embracing its scope, the city fathers of Memphis took over the Odeon and populated it with touring theatrical companies and the great musicians of the day. Over the years, the Odeon became home to singers and jugglers, great actors like Sarah Bernhardt and Edwin Booth, and renowned magicians like Howard Thurston. When the Amazing Waldo had sought a more permanent home for his Memphis tenure, the Odeon was the natural choice.

The illusionist chose it not simply for its wonderful acoustics or the generous dimensions of its stage but for the labyrinth of tunnels and storage rooms that honeycombed its depths. In designing it for productions of a grand scale like "Aida," which called for elephants and camels if it were to be properly mounted, Gustav Meyerlink had foreseen the need to build, move, and store enormous sets, legions of chariots, and multitudes of costumes. He had also provided dressing rooms for throngs of choruses to people his productions as well as lavish apartments for its star singers. He had even commissioned stables to house the livestock that might be needed one day.

All of these made perfect hiding places. Soon after he moved into the Odeon, the magician undertook to explore long-forgotten spaces beneath the old theatre. Spaces so remote along passageways so obscure that no one remembered they were there. It was to one of these remote chambers that he brought Nell Marchand.

CHAPTER 57

Wherever he had taken her was as dark as a tomb. Nell felt her way along the walls until she found the door. She tried the knob, knowing already that it would be locked. She rattled it anyway, pounded against the door with her fists, and yelled, "Let me out!" at the top of her lungs. When her hands were raw and her voice had been reduced to a croak, she slid to the floor beside the door and sat with her back against the wall. The most excruciating headache of her life threatened to split her skull. She pulled her knees up to her chin and tried to plan what she would do to him when he came for her, which he was bound to do. Unless he was going to leave her here to die alone in the dark. But she wasn't going to let herself think about that.

Where were you safe if it wasn't in the Peabody? Of course, Ellis had been shot there, but that wasn't something that happened every day.

Nell didn't have to ask who had taken her. It was Waldo. She shivered at the thought of his touching her and of being helpless in his control. Just let him get close enough to her for her to get her hands on him, and he would find out just exactly how helpless she wasn't. She might not be able to overpower him, but she would leave him with plenty to remember her for. She would claw his face to ribbons and gouge those terrible eyes of his from their sockets.

She slept, dreaming of the mayhem she would visit on the Amazing Waldo. But in her dreams, he was dressed in strange, flowing robes and wore his hair long. Joseph was there, too, dressed and coifed in the same style. She and Joseph were in a vast, colonnaded hall when Waldo appeared out of nowhere, a knife in his hand. She woke screaming.

A kerosene lamp hung by the door now threw a dim circle of light. At the center of it, seated between her and the door, watching her, was Waldo, a smile of satisfaction on his lips.

"I trust you slept well, my love."

The word "love" coming from him made her shudder, but she did her best to suppress it. "You need to get yourself up off that chair and let me out of here," Nell said.

Waldo laughed a laugh as cold as his eyes. "You always did have an imperious streak, my darling. It's part of your charm."

Nell launched herself at him, knocking the chair over and spilling Waldo onto the floor. She had just worked her thumb to the corner of his right eye when the handkerchief went over her face again, and she was out.

CHAPTER 58

Murphy appeared at Acker's door looking as though the building must be on fire. Before he could say anything, Miss Nell Marchand's driver—Jenkins—pushed past him and leaned across the sergeant's desk.

"Somebody took Miss Nell right out from under my nose," the man said.

"Took her? What are you talking about?"

Jenkins took a deep breath to steady himself. "I mean, she had me drive her down to the Peabody Hotel to pick up some pigeons from the chef, but she never came out. The chef never saw her either. Somebody took her, and y'all have got to find her."

"Sit down, and tell me everything that happened." Acker flipped to a new page on his notepad. "Murphy, tell the chief we're going to need more uniforms on the street. Nell Marchand is missing."

CHAPTER 59

Starting at the Peabody and walking tight spirals in opposite directions that crossed each other each time around, Joseph Calendar and his butler Simon set out to cover as much of downtown Memphis as possible. When Calendar reached the Odeon, it was growing dark in the city. Standing outside the theatre among the crowd that was beginning to gather for the Amazing Waldo's evening performance, Calendar felt that Nell must be there. Waldo would keep her near him, and with the performance obviously to start as scheduled, Calendar knew that the magician must have hidden her away somewhere in the theatre.

He could wait until the end of the performance and follow him, hoping that he would lead him to Nell. But Waldo might be expecting that. He was bound to know that they were looking for Nell, would have prepared for such a contingency and taken steps to safeguard himself. Did he have an accomplice? If so, there could be someone keeping watch over Nell, prepared to spring on unsuspecting searchers who came for her. Calendar would have to take great care.

Best to begin the search while Waldo was onstage. That way, Calendar could count on at least an hour to explore the theatre. He waited to join the last group to enter. Pulling his hat low over his face and his coat collar as high as he could, he hoped that even if Waldo were watching the door, he could still slip by him unnoticed. It might be a vain hope—after so many years, Waldo would probably recognize him whatever guise he assumed—but he had to grasp for every advantage that he could.

CHAPTER 60

In repose, Nell was more beautiful even than he remembered her. Without the hate in her eyes that shriveled his heart, he could imagine that she was simply asleep and that she would wake with a smile to welcome him into her arms. He'd dreamed it so a thousand times.

By now, Waldo was sure, they knew she was gone. They would be looking for her all over the city. Calendar would know he had her. Would he risk telling the police, or would he come for her himself? Waldo smiled. Calendar would come alone, and he would be waiting for him. It would be just as it had been before. Waldo ran his thumb along the edge of the ceremonial knife, testing its edge for sharpness. Next to the knife, the keenest of razors was dull.

This time, though, he would not dispatch his old enemy in front of his love. Let Nell believe that she had been abandoned. Forgotten. That Calendar could not be bothered to search for her. Careful as he had been to choose the unlikeliest rooms beneath the theatre, no one would ever find her here in the bowels of the Odeon. With time, she would grow to depend on him, and that dependence would turn into love. He had no doubt of it.

When Nell was calmer, Waldo would move her to the lavish chambers he had prepared for her. He would not be able to extend his run at the Odeon forever, of course, but by the time he had to move on, she would be ready to follow him anywhere. He would take her to Europe, show her the world. Before long, she would forget that she had ever known any other life but the one at his side.

Her eyes fluttered open, and she stared wildly around her before she remembered where she was. She tried to sit up, to fling herself at him again, but he had tied her hands together in front of her. She wiggled herself to a sitting position, her eyes so full of loathing that he almost quailed at the sight.

"You must forgive me for binding your lovely hands, my dear, but I cannot risk your attacking me again. I have no wish to harm you."

Nell clenched her fists, tested the bonds, and dropped her hands to her lap.

"That's better," Waldo said. "It's futile to fight me, you know. We have always been destined for each other, and the sooner you accept that, the better. I will give you a life of luxury and such love as you've never imagined."

"I'd rather be dead."

"No, my dear, you wouldn't. Death is such a cold place. Cold and lonely, if we are to believe Mr. Marvel. How does the line go? 'The grave's a fine and private place, but none I think do there embrace.' That's not the future you envision for yourself, is it? Lying alone through all eternity. It's certainly not one I would wish for you or myself."

Waldo uncovered a plate of fruit and cheese that he had brought and placed it next to her. "Eating will be somewhat awkward, so I've sliced these tidbits for you. Of course, if you promise to behave yourself, I can untie you."

Nell didn't answer. Instead, she reached under the edge of the plate, worked her fingers over it, and threw it in his direction.

"A proud gesture, my love, but I wonder how long it will be before you're so hungry that you'll be eating out of my hand?" He gathered up the grapes, apple slices, and bits of cheese and came to crouch beside her. He would have caressed her cheek with his free hand, but she turned her face away, clenching her teeth and squeezing her eyes closed.

"All right, Nell. I'll leave you to rest and think. You must know that I want only what's best for you. In a few minutes, I have a performance, but I'll be back afterward, and we can talk more." He rested his hand on her hair, and she shivered. "Are you chilly? Here." He set the plate down and removed his cape, which he spread over her and tucked around her shoulders. "This should keep you warm until I return. You'll be thirsty. Shall I bring us a bottle of wine to share?"

Again, she didn't answer and kept her face turned as far from him as she could.

"Very well. I'll leave the lamp for you. I know how terrifying it can be to sit alone in the dark. Think about what I've said."

When the door had closed behind him, Nell scrubbed at her cheek where his fingers had brushed against it. There wasn't enough soap in the world to wash away the evil.

CHAPTER 61

Hattie sat at the kitchen table, her plate untouched before her. Across from her, Bess Marchand, blissfully unaware of what had transpired, was sopping up the last of the pot liquor with a piece of corn bread. Replete, she sat back, sighing.

"Hattie, you have not eaten a bite of your supper. Are you feeling poorly?"

"Yes, ma'am, Miss Bess. My stomach is bothering me a little bit. I just don't feel hungry."

"You should go lie down, then. I'm not so helpless that I can't manage the dishes on my own. I wonder if you could have eaten something that didn't agree with you. I don't know what that could have been, though, because we've had the same things, and I feel just fine."

Bess Marchand had never been allowed to wash dishes, partly in deference to her age, which neither Hattie nor Nell would ever dare say to her, but also because she was something of a butterfingers who was always startled when a figurine she was dusting or a coffee cup from which she was drinking ended up in pieces on the floor. Hattie didn't like to think what might happen if she turned her loose on a whole pile of dirty dishes slippery with soap.

"That's all right, Miss Bess. There aren't many dishes to do anyway. Why don't you go on into the sitting room and get your program on the radio? I'll wash up in here."

Bess consulted the watch she kept pinned to her chest. The Judge had given it to her on their first anniversary, and she had already told

Hattie and Nell and anybody else who would listen that she wanted to be buried with that watch and her locket. "Oh, gracious, it is about time for Jack Benny. He is so funny, you know. I don't think there's anyone on the radio with a sharper wit than his, unless it's George Burns. Of course, Gracie Allen makes a better foil than Mary Livingstone, but then Mr. Benny does have Rochester. You know, I just can't make up my mind."

"Yes, ma'am. You go on, and I'll take care of the kitchen. You want me to bring you your coffee in the sitting room?"

"Oh, yes, Hattie, please. I would enjoy that so much. There's nothing like a good cup of coffee to settle a meal, don't you think?"

Bess Marchand wandered out into the hall just as Jenkins entered through the back door, looking like Death gnawing on a cracker.

Hattie's heart sank even lower than it had been. "What did the police have to say?"

Jenkins sat down at the table and removed his cap. He scrubbed at his eyes and ran his hands through his hair before he answered. "I went straight to that Sergeant Acker, just like Dr. Calendar said to do. When I told him what happened to Miss Nell, he moved like a raccoon with a pack of dogs on his tail. Wasn't two minutes before he had that whole station out looking for her. Said he'd call the house soon as they knew anything. I guess there's no news here."

Hattie put a plate of fried chicken, greens, and biscuits in front of the driver. He looked at it as though he had just about as much appetite as she did, which was none, but he picked up a chicken leg and took a big bite out of it.

"Not a mumbling word, but Dr. Calendar called in a little while ago to see if we'd heard anything. He's going to find Nell. I know he will."

"He isn't about to give up before he does. I've never seen a man love a woman more than he does Miss Nell."

Setting the butter next to Jenkins, Hattie pulled out a chair and sat beside him. "I know that's right." She shook her head. "I just hope when he does find her, he has sense enough to tell her."

CHAPTER 62

Beneath the Odeon Theatre, the labyrinth of passageways and rooms seemed endless. More than once, Joseph Calendar was sure that he had lost his way, but then the sound of the audience would grow stronger, and he knew he had turned toward the stage again. Over the decades, stage crews had stored coils of rope, boards, piles of canvas, and boxes of tools willy-nilly in the passages. The first time he tripped over a coil of rope, he had fallen with such a thud that he was sure anyone hiding beneath the theatre could hear him and had lain still, listening for footsteps. After that, he kept the beam of the flashlight trained on the floor.

Stealth was everything. If Waldo did have an accomplice, Calendar would need to take him by surprise before he could move to harm Nell or warn the magician that his hiding place had been discovered. Calendar was grateful for his training in controlling his breathing and heart rate, something the greatest illusionists could do at will. He remembered well the lesson of Houdini, who, had he not been able to control his breathing, would have died in the Detroit river trapped beneath the ice.

Houdini had always maintained that it was the sound of his mother's voice calling his name that had drawn him to the opening in the ice and safety. Calendar relaxed his mind, heightened his sense, and called out with his mind to Nell.

Where are you?

NELL WAS DREAMING AGAIN. SHE RAN THROUGH THE COLONNADED hall, looking for Joseph but unable to find him. At each corner, she paused, sure that he must be just around it. Behind her, she could hear Waldo's footsteps, and she sprinted.

Where are you? She heard Joseph calling her.

"Here, Joseph. I'm here."

She opened her eyes, but she was back in the room, alone. The lamp burned over her head, and Waldo's chair still lay on its side where she had toppled it.

"I'm here," she said again, softly this time. She knew he couldn't hear her.

ON THE STAGE ABOVE THEM, THE AMAZING WALDO WAS ABOUT TO SAW his latest lovely assistant in half. The buxom waitress from the diner was much less troublesome than Penelope had been, and she cleaned up real nice, as the locals liked to say. As long as Minnie didn't open her mouth, she gave an illusion of elegance and grace. He had yet to decide if he would take her with him when he left Memphis—Nell might be jealous—but for now, his assistant was intrepid enough to submit to any illusion he proposed.

The house had grown quiet just before the saw was about to enter the slot that would guide it on its downward path. It was so still in the theatre that Waldo could hear Minnie breathing in and out only a little more quickly than usual. Although he had explained carefully to her how the trick worked, he wasn't sure she had understood. She was afraid but only a little. Trusting child.

Ears straining, he paused. Did he hear a faint voice calling "I'm here"? He waited, but it did not come again. Must have been his imagination. He made his first cut with the saw, and several members of the audience gasped. The applause that burst out when he had finished and Minnie stood to show everyone that she was still in one piece drowned out any other sound. Still, it would be best to check on Nell as soon as the show was over and prepare to lie in wait for Calendar and for his revenge.

CHAPTER 63

Arnold Acker had never trusted the magician, no matter how many alibis he provided. When Jenkins told him that Joseph Calendar was sure Waldo had kidnapped her, the sergeant felt vindicated. With every available Memphis beat cop and detective out on the street looking for Nell Marchand, he decided that he and Murphy would confront the Amazing Waldo themselves.

"Head over to the Odeon," he said to Murphy, who was behind the wheel of the Ford.

"You think he's got Mrs. Marchand, too, don't you? What would he want with a society lady like her?"

"We've got to check out every possibility. It's hard to believe even Waldo is that crazy, but I just want to be sure."

"Yes, sir, Sarge."

When they pulled up outside the Odeon, it was obvious that a performance was under way.

Cold-blooded bastard. If Waldo did have Nell Marchand, he must have ice water in his veins if he could still go on with his show. Lord have mercy, Acker just hoped that didn't mean he had killed her.

He and Murphy entered the back of the theatre, flashing their badges at the usher who would have stopped them. The man's eyes bugged for a moment, then he led them to the spot reserved for standing-room-only ticket holders. A middle-aged woman and what looked like 15 teenage girls shuffled over to make room for the policemen.

Up on stage, Waldo had just extracted his assistant from some kind of case in which he had apparently successfully sawn her in half without injuring her.

"That's a different girl," Murphy whispered out of the side of his mouth. "Last time I was here, he had this little-bitty blonde named Penelope up on stage with him. I reckon we'd better be looking for her, too, before this is all over."

Acker nodded, his eyes fixed on the stage.

"Where's his cape?" Murphy said.

"What?"

"He's usually got this dark cape that's covered with gold stars. Uses it in his act. I don't see it anywhere. What if he put it over the body?"

One of the girls standing next to the officer looked over anxiously and shuffled a couple of steps further away from him.

"Murphy, shut your mouth, boy," Acker said.

"Yes, sir."

The magician paused, looking out over the audience with his head cocked to one side like an animal that senses a threat but can't locate it. Scanning the theatre, he locked eyes with Acker and smiled.

The sergeant shivered. "He's got her all right. I just hope to God we're not too late."

THE GAME, AS CONAN DOYLE'S DETECTIVE WAS FOND OF SAYING, WAS afoot.

The uncannily tall police sergeant Acker stood in plain sight at the back of the theatre, his short, round companion no doubt somewhere at his side. Waldo saw him and knew at once that he was not there for the performance. The alert must have gone out that Nell Marchand was missing.

The magician was a little surprised that Joseph Calendar had involved the police. He had expected the medium to come alone, taking up the challenge once again. Waldo had no doubt that he was already there, if not among the audience in the theatre, then below it, searching for Nell. Facing his old nemesis and the police at the same time could only add spice to his little amusement.

The presence of the police might mean, however, that he and Nell would have to leave Memphis right away. Even if he persuaded them that he knew nothing of her disappearance, they would be watching him. And now Calendar would disappear as well. No, things would become more uncomfortable than he was willing to endure. The Amazing Waldo did not like to be inconvenienced.

He would return to Chicago while he decided the course of their life together. The theatre there could guarantee him an extended run, and it would be easier to keep Nell hidden in a larger city. Who knows? He might even call on Matilda to see if she had married her butcher yet.

Meanwhile, there was a performance to complete. He signaled to the stagehands to roll the Egyptian case to the center of the stage. He stepped to the edge until he was awash in the glow of the footlights. "Ladies and gentlemen, is there anyone among you who dares the greatest illusion of the evening? I ask only that you step into this ancient coffin, once resting place of Imhotep the Great, master magician of Egypt, where I will make you disappear. If you will only trust yourself to my care, I promise there is no danger."

CHAPTER 64

This time, Nell knew she was awake and that it was Joseph's voice she heard calling her name.

"Nell, where are you?"

She scooted closer to the door. "Here, Joseph. I'm here."

Outside, she heard his footsteps approach, pass, and turn back.

"I'm in here."

The knob turned first one way and then the other. "It's locked. You're going to have to break it down."

There was a scrabbling sound at the lock, and then Joseph was beside her, untying her hands.

"How did you do that?"

He held up a slender implement that she recognized as a pick. Bess had a weakness for mysteries, and every time a new one came to the picture show, they went to see it. Movie detectives always seemed to be picking locks to the doors of enigmatic houses.

"There have been times in my life that bolted doors have been an inopportuneness that I could ill afford. Are you hurt?" He took her face between his hands and peered at her, concern furrowing his brow and the corners of his mouth.

"No, but he drugged me with something to get me here. He used it again when I tried to fight him. I did try to fight, Joseph."

"I know you did, brave girl. He probably used chloroform on you. It renders a subject unconscious within seconds."

"Is it wicked, evil-smelling stuff that makes your head hurt like the devil afterward?"

"Yes."

"Then that's what he used. But, quick, let's get out of here before Waldo comes back. The show must be about over."

Calendar shook his head. "No. It's safer for us to wait for him here where we can prepare ourselves. If there's even a chance we could lose our way in these passages, he'll have the advantage. He's had days to explore them. We'll hear him coming, and we'll be ready for him."

"What are you going to do?"

"Dispatch him the minute he steps through that door. Snap his neck. I'll have the advantage of surprise." Calendar closed the door and used the pick to secure it. He tested the knob to be sure it had, indeed, locked and nodded to himself in satisfaction. "He won't know I've found you yet. If I put out the lamp, he'll be coming from light into darkness. Before he knows I'm here and prepares himself, I'll finish him."

"You know how to break a man's neck?"

Calendar paused. "That's another skill I've had to acquire over the years. I've been in tight spots before." He squeezed her hand. "Now, get as far from the door as you can. No matter what happens, stay back. If I'm worrying where you are, that you'll be hurt, I won't be able to concentrate on the task at hand. Promise me you'll stay out of the way."

"All right, Joseph." Nell took up a position across the room, her back pressed into the farthest corner. She thought about asking him what kind of tight spots he'd been in that required snapping a man's neck to extract himself, but she decided she didn't really want to know.

"Ready?" he asked, taking the lamp down from its hook.

She nodded.

Calendar blew out the lamp, and again they were plunged into darkness.

CHAPTER 65

The last audience members were trailing out of the theatre when Waldo spotted Acker and Murphy approaching the stage. He decided that entertaining as it might be, he did not want to take the time to speak with them just now. The police could wait. Now, he must go to Nell and prepare himself for the confrontation with Calendar. For all he knew, the medium might already have found her, slim as the chances were and well-hidden as she was. Still, it was best to be sure.

Waldo made his way out of the wings and down the back stairs. He slipped behind the curtain that hid the entrance to the oldest passageways, moving quickly and silently so the police would not be able to detect which way he had gone. For the first five minutes, he made his way in darkness lest the light give him away. When he felt sure that no one followed, he turned on the flashlight and hurried toward the room where he had hidden Nell.

Here and there along the way, he saw signs that someone had passed. It must be Calendar, stumbling blind and lost. But for Waldo, the passages were like the footpaths he'd run as a boy back on his grandparents' farm in Ohio. He knew them just as well, better, perhaps, for having studied them so carefully.

He had chosen the most inaccessible corner of the old storage rooms in which to hide his prize. Arriving at her door, he saw that light no longer shone from beneath it. The lamp should have held enough kerosene to keep it burning for hours. There was a chance that she'd managed to reach it, even with her hands bound. She could be waiting on the other side of the door, ready to swing it down on his head when he entered.

Waldo tried the doorknob. Still locked. Good. He could lie in wait for Calendar to come.

"You know, Nell, there's no use resisting me," he said through the closed door. "I'm stronger than you are, and now I know you're waiting for me. Are you considering braining me with the lamp? You'll simply be wasting your effort."

No answer, but then he hadn't expected one. He pressed his ear against the door, listening for sounds of her moving into position on the other side. Nothing.

Waldo took the key from his pocket and unlocked the door. He pushed it open and stepped back in case she lunged for him when he entered. Not a movement from within. Cautiously, he stepped to the door and shined the light around the room. There she was, backed into a corner, shielding her dark-accustomed eyes from the light that played across her face. Shielding them with her now-unbound hands.

"Ah, what a clever girl. I see that you have managed to free your hands. Perhaps I should have bound them behind you instead. Of course, if you'll agree to behave yourself, it won't be necessary to tie you at all. You're mine now, and you may as well accept it."

Stretching out a placating hand toward her, Waldo stepped into the room.

Behind him, the door squeaked on its hinges. Before he could turn to meet the assault, Calendar was on him, knocking him to his knees and sending the flashlight skittering across the floor. Still, Waldo managed to turn his torso and parry the attack so that his enemy overshot him. As he passed, the magician brought his elbow up, striking him across the Adam's apple with all the force he could muster.

Calendar stumbled and sprawled onto his back, choking. Waldo scrambled over, planting a knee against the fallen man's breastbone and bringing the heel of his hand sharply down on his throat again. He must seize the advantage while he had him down. Waldo reached for the back waistband of his trousers, his hand closing on the knife.

CHAPTER 66

The light rolled to Nell's feet, and she grabbed it, sweeping the beam over the room until the light played over the grappling men. The magician had Joseph on his back and now held a knife aloft, ready to strike home. The blood of her Welsh warrior and Confederate cavalry ancestors boiled up in her veins. Grasping the flashlight in both hands, she raised it over her head and charged Waldo where he had Calendar pinned. She crashed the torch down on the magician's skull, and the crack of metal on bone resounded through the room.

Dropping the blade, Waldo goggled up at Nell as Goliath must have gawped at David when the fatal stone from the boy shepherd's sling found its mark. The magician tried to roll away, but she came after him, striking the side of his head and sending him flying against the wall. Battering his head and shoulders and every part of him she could reach, she hefted the flashlight again and again. A terrible banshee keening filled her ears that she realized issued from her mouth. Waldo no longer resisted or moved, but still she struck him with the now-slippery instrument.

Then, Calendar was beside her, catching her wrists as she raised her arms again. "Nell. Stop. Nell! He's dead, darling. Stop. He's dead." He eased the battered flashlight from her hands, dropped it, and pulled her into the sanctuary of his embrace.

"Joseph!" Nell found his face with her fingers, ran her hands over his shoulders, touched his hair. "Are you all right? He was going to kill you. I had to stop him. I had to stop him."

221

"I know, my darling. You did. You stopped him. I am not injured."

She buried her hands in his hair, drew his mouth to hers, and kissed him, fierce with terror and relief. He kissed her back, holding her close until she thought she would faint or die from the joy of it. Murmuring her name, he swept his lips down her neck, searing her flesh everywhere they touched.

"Miss Nell!" The shout and the sound of running feet came from the hallway.

He released her, smoothed her hair from her face, and stepped back. "Answer them."

"Joseph." She reached for him.

"It's all right, Nell. There will be time, my love. There will be time."

"Here, Arnold! We're in here."

Arnold Acker burst through the doorway, another man hot on his heels. They played their flashlights over the room until they found her, standing bereft and unutterably weary.

"Miss Nell," the sergeant said, moving toward her. "Thank the Lord we found you."

"All the saints in heaven," Officer Murphy said.

Nell looked down and realized that she was covered in Waldo's blood.

CHAPTER 67

"Arnold, please pull up under the porte cochère," Nell said. "I don't want anyone to see me like this. We'll go in through the back door."

After she had assured them all that she was not hurt and that she wanted to go home, the sergeant had insisted on driving her himself.

"Yes, ma'am. And if you don't feel like coming down to the station for a day or two, it can wait. Waldo Peterfreund isn't going anywhere."

Nell shivered and leaned against Joseph Calendar, who put his arm around her. She didn't care if Arnold Acker did shoot them a look in his rearview mirror. Whatever he thought about the two of them, he had sense enough to keep it to himself.

At the house, Calendar held the kitchen door open for her. She stepped inside and saw Hattie and Jenkins keeping vigil at the table.

"Nell!" Hattie said at the sight of her. The cook streaked across the kitchen to grab her by the shoulders and turn her this way and that. "Oh, baby girl, he did hurt you."

"No, Hattie. I'm all right. I just want to get this dress off me and take a bath."

"All right, baby. We'll take you on upstairs and get you out of it. I'll fill the tub with scalding hot water, just like you like it."

Reaching back her hand, Nell looked over her shoulder at Calendar. "Joseph, you'll stay, won't you?"

"As long as you want me to." He took her hand.

"Hattie, please be sure there's plenty of soap. And burn this dress. I don't want to look at it ever again. Burn it, and Jenkins, you carry away the ashes."

CHAPTER 68

At the kitchen table, Calendar sat with Nell, drinking brandy. Jenkins had gone to his room over the garage, and Bess Marchand had also retired. She had been spared the sight of a blood-drenched Nell but had still required several liberal slugs of brandy herself to calm her during the recounting of what had happened at the Odeon. Nell was on her second cup of hot chocolate laced with bourbon and had finally stopped shivering.

"He's dead, Joseph. It's over. My Lord in heaven, that's the worst thing I've ever been through in my life."

"Yes, Nell." He did not tell her that it was very likely not over, that it wasn't the worst thing she had ever endured. It was simply the worst thing she could remember. He reached for her hand. "Darling, I–"

"Don't." She looked over at Hattie, who was washing the chocolate pan at the sink and pretending not to listen. "I can't talk about it tonight. There's time, just as you said. Why don't you go on upstairs? I want to be quiet here for a while longer. Hattie has the blue bedroom ready for you."

"As you wish." He leaned toward her, thought better of it, and kissed her hand instead. "I'll see you in the morning."

As soon as the medium closed the kitchen door behind him, Hattie came to stand over Nell, the dish towel still in her hand.

"You know, if you don't watch out, one of these days Dr. Calendar might get tired of waiting for you. Then what you going to do?"

Putting her fingers to her lips where after all these hours his kiss still burned, Nell smiled.

THE END

ABOUT THE AUTHOR

The author of award-winning novels and screenplays, Jane Sevier began her career as a feature writer. She covered fields as varied as artificial intelligence and the arts and traveled on assignment to exotic locales as diverse as Ecuador, Sri Lanka, and Texarkana, Texas. Several of her feature stories garnered national and regional recognition.

Jane loves travel and has lived in Dallas; Paris; Washington, D.C.; Austin; and Nashville. An 8th-generation Tennessean, she will always be a true child of the South, no matter where she hangs her hat. Visit Jane at www.janesevier.com.